NEW YORK REVIEW BOOKS
CLASSICS

AFTER CLAUDE

IRIS OWENS (née Klein) (?–2008) was born and raised in New York City, the daughter of a professional gambler. She attended Barnard College, was briefly married, and then moved to Paris, where she fell in with Alexander Trocchi, the editor of the legendary avant-garde journal *Merlin* and a notorious heroin addict, and supported herself by producing pornography (under the name of Harriet Daimler) for Maurice Girodias's Olympia Press. Back in the United States, Owens wrote *After Claude*, which came out in 1973. A second novel, *Hope Diamond Refuses*, loosely based on her marriage to an Iranian prince, was published in 1984.

EMILY PRAGER is a novelist, a Literary Lion of the New York Public Library, and the winner of the Columbia Graduate School of Journalism 2000 Online Journalism Award for Commentary. She is at work on a book of essays for Random House, entitled *Secrets of Shanghai*.

AFTER CLAUDE

IRIS OWENS

Introduction by
EMILY PRAGER

NEW YORK REVIEW BOOKS

New York

THIS IS A NEW YORK REVIEW BOOK
PUBLISHED BY THE NEW YORK REVIEW OF BOOKS
435 Hudson Street, New York, NY 10014
www.nyrb.com

Library of Congress Cataloging-in-Publication Data
Owens, Iris.
After Claude / by Iris Owens ; introduction by Emily Prager.
    p. cm. — (New York Review Books classics)
Originally published: New York : Farrar, Straus and Giroux, 1973.
ISBN 978-1-59017-363-3 (alk. paper)
1. Greenwich Village (New York, N.Y.)—Fiction. 2. Chick lit. I. Title.
PS3554.A3A69 2010
813'.54—dc22

                    2010022565

ISBN 978-1-59017-363-3

Printed in the United States of America on acid-free paper.
10 9 8 7 6 5 4 3 2 1

INTRODUCTION

I AM honored to write this introduction for Iris's book but I think you should know she and I were not speaking. When you read *After Claude*, you will understand how perfect this actually is—what a stroke of genius on the part of fate and her evil handmaiden, literary criticism, that I should be the one chosen to discuss her in print, and postmortem at that, but then it was through writing about Iris's work that I first encountered Iris—in 1984, I reviewed her second novel, *Hope Diamond Refuses*, favorably, for *The New York Times*.

We had a mutual friend, the satirist Lynn Phillips, who introduced us after that, and I recall quite clearly walking over to Iris's apartment in the Village, where we both lived, meeting her, and then spending the next nine hours on her sofa laughing hysterically. We had things in common. We were both humorists, bohemians, and intellectuals, and we were trying to live in the '80s in New York City, which, between cocaine and AIDS, was a period of such frothing shallowness mixed with such bone-crushing sadness that it was an unending font of human mortification—a state which we both revered deeply.

I did not know much about Iris's days with the Olympia Press in Paris but my father did, and he was impressed that I met her. My father was exactly that American soldier that Maurice Girodias was out to target in 1953 when he enlisted the twenty-year-old Iris and other writers for the literary magazine *Merlin* in creating pornography to make some money. Girodias christened her Harriet Daimler and, under this pseudonym, she went on to write six novels for his Traveller's Companion series. The most famous of these, *Darling*, is a lengthy and rather vicious rape fantasy, which makes sense since the conundrum of rape—that in fantasy it's a turn-on but in reality a horrific nightmare—was the kind of female madness that Iris was interested in.

We never talked about her stint at the Olympia Press because in those days it was quite common for humorists to have gotten their start in pornographic books or magazines, particularly black humorists because, and this is so hard to believe now it's like saying we all once owned horses, until the '70s, really, you could not talk or write about sex in public, much less make fun of it, without being arrested or charged with witchcraft. But shady publications welcomed us with open legs.

Reading *After Claude* again, I was struck by how much the main character, Harriet, resembles Iris in kind of a hyperbolic way. Iris had, like Harriet, an incredibly Semitic beauty—"exotic cheekbones, you'd wonder what Egyptian tomb had been pilfered"—and a brilliant intelligence which manifested in a devastating napalm-like wit. She was the mistress of understatement. Reading throwaway lines like "as an American my war against injustice knows no bounds" brings me right back to sitting on the couch with her. And like Harriet, Iris preferred life to just take its course, accepted being sometimes mangled in its wake, and truly enjoyed hanging out.

It is in Harriet's fathomless neediness, in her manic desperation to find a man, any man to barnacle on to, that the fiction appears, because when I knew her, Iris was a loner. There was always some genius, creative guy mooning around her, and, true, she had been married twice and loved a party, but because of her insistence on honesty mixed with a very gentle sweetness, she had a love/hate relationship with humanity; as Harriet puts it, hers "was a large and generous nature, and, therefore, it [was] not like [her] to notice how base practically everyone is."

After Claude is the hilarious story of a breakup as it takes place in the dissolving mind of a brilliantly funny, parasitic ne'er-do well. But it is also a withering statement about intelligence in women. On the one hand, Harriet says, "I have . . . learned never to be amazed at what men will resort to when cornered by a woman's intelligence," a sentiment with which any feminist of salt could agree. On the other hand, Harriet also says, referring to Claude whom she doesn't love, "I reached up and grabbed his arm, clinging to it as though it were the overhanging branch between me and the fatal drop," as if she cannot even think of how to survive without him. This predilection of bright women to twist themselves into bizarre submissive postures from which only humor can release them is something die-hard feminists will never address. But Iris and I were in agreement: there is nothing that warms a smart girl's heart like a smile on the face of a sadist.

Throughout the book, Harriet is psychologically paralyzed. Whether from depression, mononucleosis, or mind-numbing laziness, she stays in bed most of the day, watches daytime quiz shows, and seems to be on a quest to accomplish as little as possible. Even when Claude finally throws her out of the house, she is instantly thumbing the next free ride, and when she flags down Roger the guru at the Chelsea Hotel, she's ready to climb right on board despite his rather blistering account of the domination that awaits her at the hands of his boss, the Mansonesque Victor. "You mean nobody has to work," she crows, singling out the most salient point of his discussion of the commune. "Living is our work," he replies to her delighted relief.

It occurred to me as I read that Harriet's paralysis might be a veiled allusion to Iris's struggle with writing. She was one of those writers who hates doing the writing and avoids it like the plague and is tortured night and day by the specter of what should be written. This was, of course, in large measure due to the perfection she required of her jokes and the perceptions behind them, "the terrible isolation of integrity" Harriet calls it, as well as to the extreme sensitivity she needed to produce them, a sensitivity which makes Harriet's descent into madness at once excruciatingly funny, all too familiar, and terribly scary. Iris's preference for the fast, exciting ingestion of life rather than its painful, drawn-out, solo regurgitation is something with which I can well identify. If every woman's fears and frailties can be hysterically articulated in one book, this is it.

I asked Lynn Phillips for her favorite joke of Iris's. "My personal favorite," she e-mailed, "was from a write-in interview of downtown New York City authors in that neighborhood newspaper, *The Villager*. The question put to the interviewees was, 'What was the biggest lie you have ever been told?' The other writers gave answers like, 'The check is in the mail,' and 'This won't get you pregnant.' But Iris's answer was, 'Work will make you free.'

"It was a joke about the American dream," Lynn continued. "It was a joke about being Jewish. (The Nazis erected a sign at the gates of Auschwitz reading, *Arbeit macht frei*, or 'work makes freedom.') It was a joke about writer's block. (When your standards of psychological honesty were as strict as hers, impending deadlines feel like advancing storm troopers.) More, it was a joke about the second-wave feminist delusion that entering the workforce would somehow liberate women from male domination—rather than simply changing the signage. On top of those jokes, there is also, of course, the joke of finding career coaches, the Nazis, literary agents and feminists telling her the same lie. But the biggest joke of all is the tacit puzzle that underlies it . . . if work won't make you free, what will?"

One time I took a friend of mine over to meet Iris. She was a French-Canadian girl, very pretty in a kind of *Little Women* way, an affect she summoned up by wearing

Victorian-inspired clothes. She was one of those girls who looks like a child but has a mind like a steel trap. She was an agent in the music business and one of the first people I knew to make money playing the market on the Internet. We were talking about pool parties and she suddenly confessed that she hated them because she didn't particularly care for her legs. Iris stopped dead and turned to her. "Are you looking for perfection?" she asked.

After Claude is definitely a meditation on the ends to which intelligent women will resort not to use their intelligence. But the latter half of the book is a scorching lampoon of the 1970s everyone-loves-each-other gooey groupthink that made the period so fertile for con men. But here, Victor, the cult leader, and his pathologically understanding lackey, Roger, are also in danger. "It's been a long time, many moons, since a chick pulled me into her movie," Roger snorts, leaving one wondering whether he has an inkling of what he and Victor might be getting themselves into if they seduce and recruit Harriet.

I can't remember exactly why Iris and I weren't speaking, but I know I was in good company. Over the years Iris found herself no longer on speaking terms with all sorts of friends, including Samuel Beckett, Susan Sontag, Pauline Kael, Ad Reinhardt, Rudy Wurlitzer, and Robert Mapplethorpe. Iris liked smart company. I believe she accused me of stealing her joke or something, and I was so outraged by the fact that she would accuse me of such a thing that I flounced out of her apartment and, before we knew it, years had passed. But the truth is that right before it happened I became a mother, and suddenly it wasn't easy to hang out and time was scarce and babysitters required. (One of the more interesting revelations of parenthood is with which of your friends you would pay to have dinner.)

My relationship with Iris was too delicate to become casual. It was like a jazz riff that needed to spin out over hours, to build and build to the perfect rejoinder, the one possible topper in the elusive but celestial humorous rhythm. You had to be good, really good. That's how Iris liked it.

One night, late into the evening in the early '90s, we were, I admit, blasted, and laughing like crazy when Iris went dead serious. She fixed me with her smart, black eyes and gave me some advice I have followed to this day. "Whenever you feel yourself wanting to do good," she said somberly, "run in the opposite direction."

—EMILY PRAGER

AFTER CLAUDE

To the memory of my parents

I wish to thank the management of the Hotel Chelsea for permitting me to use and describe the hotel with all the fictional liberties necessary to the characters and action of the book. The Chelsea has long been a haven for a distinguished list of creative people, since it supports and encourages artistic expression with a humanity rare in New York, or any city. It is a tribute to the Chelsea that it will not interfere with that expression, even when made its victim, and I hope the residents, past, present, and future, will forgive the narrator's excesses regarding the celebrated New York landmark.

IRIS OWENS

I LEFT Claude, the French rat. Six months of devotion wasted on him was more than enough. I left him as the result of an argument we had over a lousy movie, a sort of Communist version of Christ's life, except it didn't seem Communistic to me, whatever that is. Everyone was poor all right, and Mary didn't sport her diamond tiara, but otherwise it was the same old religious crap about how wonderful it is to be a pauper after you're dead. It took them a good half hour to nail Christ to this authentic cross with wooden pegs and a wooden mallet, thump thump, nice and slow so if your thing happens to be palmistry you could become the world's leading authority on the fortunes of Jesus Christ. Then, in case we thought we were watching a routine crucifixion, the sky turned black, thunder and lightning, the Roman troops, played by Yugoslavia's renowned soccer team, squirmed around on their picnic blankets, pondering whether to throw the dice or pack it up.

"Do you think they'll have to call off the game?" I nudged my French boy friend, which was when I saw that the idiot was having himself a full-blown Catholic seizure.

Claude glowered at me, and in the gloom of the theater, conveniently illuminated by the flashes of divine lightning occurring on the screen, I got a strobe picture of his features: dark, intense frog eyes, abundant black curly hair foaming out of his head, and finally, his full lips, sealed in a hurt pout. Claude had two expressions: that one, which accompanied his profound moods, and the other one, sleepy eyes, mouth relaxed and puffed as if he were blowing out invisible candles, which was the face he woke up with and starred in most of the day.

He might have answered me, but all human exchange was drowned in a clout of heavenly thunder that simultaneously wiped out Christ and the critical faculties of the stunned audience. The houselights went up, and I found myself in this ward of catatonics.

"Thank God," I said, as we staggered toward the aisle. "I thought that fag would never die." You can't imagine the looks I got from the shell-shock victims. Claude, who wasn't in such great shape himself, made a dazed push for the door.

We left the theater with the rest of the zombies and filed out into the hell of Manhattan's Upper West Side, me wondering how I had allowed Claude to con me into penetrating enemy territory for the privilege of undergoing that exquisite torture. It was hot, New York summer hot, the airless streets pressure-cooked into a thick layer of grease and scum, which reminded me of the best part of the movie which was that it had been cool in there. I lit my first Marlboro in three hours, since the so-called art house considered it very unartistic to smoke anywhere but in the balcony, and Claude, a non-smoker, was happy only in the third row of the orchestra. As a film connoisseur, he deemed it his duty to sit as close to the screen as his neck muscles would tolerate.

"Boy," I said, drawing the smoke into my deprived lungs, "it's all fixed or the guy who invented air conditioning would certainly have won the Academy Award by now."

"Why the hell don't you ever shut up? It's a drag to take you anywhere."

I gathered from Claude's tone that I had committed a crime, but the only offense I could think of was that of retaining my sanity throughout the endless dirge.

Claude, who had learned his English in England, spoke with one of those snotty, superior accents, stuffed into a slimy French accent, the whole mess flavored with an occasional American hipsterism, making him sound like an extremely rich, self-employed spy. I forgive myself for not instantly despising him, because one: it's not my style to pass hasty judgments on people, and two: it was my luck to meet him under circumstances that made anyone not holding a knife to my throat look appealing.

All around us, the shuffling movie patrons seemed to be snapping out of their trances, because a babble of words rose out of them, and instead of mounting into a riot, instead of rushing back into the theater and pulling up the rows of moth-eaten seats, there was just this Greek chorus about how authentic, how beautiful their recent ordeal had been.

"Authentic," I snorted at Claude. "What makes the director so sure Christ had rotten teeth and acne?" Because, believe me, his close-ups had been unsparing.

"Shut up. Stop attracting attention. It's embarrassing to take you anywhere."

"What is it with you, Claude? Can't we go to a crummy movie without you getting hysterical about the impression I'm making?"

Claude marched smartly ahead of me, and I was practically running, as well as shouting, to keep in touch with him. In a normal neighborhood, we might have aroused suspicion, but up there, it just passed as a harmless purse snatching.

"Slow up," I yelled, when he reached the corner of Broadway and Ninety-fifth Street, because it's not one of my favorite fantasies to be abducted by six muscular militants to go play White Goddess in the back room of guerrilla headquarters. Claude waited, but not necessarily for me. He was searching nervously up and down the hostile streets. I knew he was having a crisis about whether to spend three dollars plus on a taxi ride down to the Village or to risk a knifing/mugging expedition on the IRT, a soul-searching choice for a Frenchman to make.

"Decide, sweetheart," I said, when I caught up to him. "Your money or your life?"

Claude pretended not to hear me, an act of male intelligence that never fails to impress me, and waved at a cab with a glowing off-duty sign. Since we were obviously desirable tenants, uncluttered by kids, pets, or luggage, the taxi came to a screeching halt at the corner. Any halfwit knows that New York taxis don't back up, so we did the hundred-yard dash like two grateful hitchhikers. There followed a brief but searching interview which established that we were all going in the same general direction. The sullen driver unlocked the back door, and Claude shoved me inside and proceeded to give the most detailed directions to our residence on Morton Street, all in his greasy headwaiter's accent, lest, God forbid, the bandit employ his own initiative and take us down the cool, quick extravagance of the West Side Highway. One additional dime spent in a taxi was Claude's idea of death by fire. The driver, hate in his heart, went careening down Broadway as if he were rushing plasma to a beheading.

What with the drenching heat, the harrowing race, and the agony of the meter ticking away Claude's lifeblood, our night might have had a peaceful dissolve into grief and silence, but being as I am the plaything of an infantile god, I found myself not in the usual filthy junk heap but in a portable crypt. Our driver, a full fanatic, had festooned the dashboard and windshield with thorned Christs, weeping Marys, pierced dripping hearts, and a display of blue wax flowers that you wouldn't want to put on your mother's grave. Scattered amidst the gore was the family album. Framed photographs of assorted mental defectives, smiling cripples, consumptives, and proudly uniformed degenerates, all looking straight ahead with the fixed stares of hostages facing a firing squad.

Since I am essentially a lighthearted person who tries to see the humor in this freak show called life, I jabbed Claude in the ribs and said, "Who do you suppose he has buried under the seat?"

"That's not funny," Claude answered, holding himself grimly in the throes of his recent religious exaltation. Claude kept his classic profile, which he tended to think of as a work of art transported across the ocean for the elevation of American females, turned away from me. He stared out the window, his heavy lids dropped over his dark eyes, the streetlights and headlights fleetingly reflected in the narrow slits between his long eyelashes.

"I didn't intend it to be funny. I intended it to be deep and tragic, like that deep and tragic movie that's destroyed your mind."

It appeared that we weren't going to embark on a stimulating discussion of why certain directors should be shot, so I leaned back on the cracked plastic cushions and lit a Marlboro. Go know you're not allowed to smoke in a hearse. At the first hint of smoke, the driver whirled around and fixed his mean, crazy, little eyes on me.

"Lady, can't you read signs?"

The fact is I can't, but even if I could, it would have taken an Indian scout to spot a sign in his jungle of relics. He helped me out by pointing to a small printed announcement stapled to his sunvisor which dealt, in essence, with the driver's medical condition and the diagnosis that he would die from the cigarette you smoked. However, what really influenced me was a tattoo on his thick, hairy forearm that I had somehow overlooked. It was a blue tombstone floating in a red cross, inscribed, "In Memory of My Dear Mother," and under that the precise date on which he had killed her. Needless to say, I didn't wish to offend anyone in such perpetual mourning, so I flipped the cigarette out the window.

"Good," Claude said, with a short, nasty laugh.

It was all too much, and I felt my divine patience wearing thin. "What is it with you?" I demanded. "Why are you being so goddamn hostile tonight? Did I ask to come to this funeral? Or, for that matter, did I ask to go to that fag movie? Yes, fag," I emphasized into his rigid profile.

"Get off me," he muttered. "It's bloody hot, and I can't breathe with you screaming obscenities into my face."

"Who's screaming? Who's being obscene? Since when did fag become obscene? Yesterday it was your favorite word." I felt entitled to say that because, according to Claude, everyone, with the possible exception of his heroes Mick Jagger and Mao Tse-tung, was a fag.

"Ugh," I said, "are you defending the movie? All those muscle men floating around in their bathrobes, clutching at each other, and that hairy, rough trade ape, John the Baptist, the way his insane eyes lit up when he spotted Christ coyly dipping into the Jordan? If you want my opinion, I think Christ should have flung back his ringlets and dived into John's caveman sarong, slurp slurp, which would have made it a more gripping movie and, for my money, more authentic, too."

Now, Claude is one of these men who think no answer is the most eloquent answer of all. Why use words is his motto, when you have eyebrows to raise, lips to tighten, and an array of Gregory Peck facial tics to express all human intelligence? It was my job to divine the precise meanings of his various spasms, which was hard work in a well-lighted living room but slavery in the confines of a darkened taxicab. Not that Claude didn't enjoy the sound of his own voice. Don't misunderstand me. He could talk for hours, days, but only on carefully selected topics, such as every disappointing course of his most recent meal. But discourse? Converse? Exchange ideas? Never, and certainly not with that brain-damaged segment of the population called women.

"Speaking of women," I moved in closer to facilitate face reading, "how'd you like Mary? Wasn't she swell? So quiet, so sad, so refined. Never pushing Jesus to become a dentist, make something of himself. In fact, now that I think of it, did she have a single line in the picture?"

Claude's reply came through his perfect, white, clenched teeth.

"I told you to get the fuck off me." A request which was declined, not by me but by the driver, who slammed on his brakes in order to avoid hitting a station wagon that had cravenly stopped for a red light. I was flung across Claude's chest.

"Will you tell that maniac to slow down?"

Claude gave me his rotten smile, as if to suggest that he and the cab driver had partaken of an immortality pill, and fastidiously rubbed the front of his shirt, where my touch had contaminated him.

"Tell him yourself. What is this sudden timidity? Am I the only person you feel free to yell at and insult?" Claude, his eyes glued to the meter, was stuttering with rage.

"Who's insulting you? That's very interesting. You treat me like I'm a leper and tell me *I'm* insulting *you*. The only insult I'm aware of was made to J. Christ, assuming that he wasn't a Jewish mama's boy, willing to go to any lengths to get out from under Mary's potato latkes. Of course he had an especially heavy problem, with her wrapping her head in blankets and swearing he was conceived in her ear. Honestly, Claude, if I were a Catholic, I'd picket the theater."

"But you're not Catholic, are you?" He turned a furious face to me. "You're just Harriet, wonderful Harriet with the big Jewish mouth." Scratch a Frenchman and find a German storm trooper.

"Jewish! Since when did my mouth become Jewish?"

If there's one slur I resent, it's having my personal powers, good or bad, credited to a factor over which I have no control. If my mouth is so Jewish, then pray tell me why my Jewish parents have never understood one single statement I've made to them? The only possible explanation is that I was stolen from the Cossacks at an impressionable age and artfully trained by my Jewish kidnappers to suffer from frequent heartburn and moronic motion pictures.

I forced myself to disregard Claude's irrelevant attack and focus on what could really be upsetting him. I knew he was upset. I hadn't spent six grueling months catering to Claude's sexual appetites without having a pretty good idea of the pervert's moods. Furthermore, he'd been having these childish tantrums for the past two weeks. Curiously enough, two weeks was the longest stretch of unbroken time that Claude and I had spent together, since his job as assistant director of a French Television news crew kept him hopping around the country. That was a clue, but what did it mean? I didn't want to face the depressing possibility that two weeks with the same woman created a sexual and emotional threat that Claude simply could not meet. The wretched movie seemed my only available opening into Claude's dilemma. I figured if we could come to some agreement about the film, we could go on from there to the real issues.

"Claude darling, let's not waste our breath on that piece of garbage. Admit you were as bored as I. I mean, two solid hours of crawling, trudging, groaning, it could depress even a normal person. Everyone mumbling and dragging around like a pack of junkies. And Salome's dance. I ask you? Every religious sect agrees it was a sexy dance, but Mr. Authentic is so determined to stupefy his public that he finds a pudgy twelve-year-old that your raving child molester would scorn, he stuffs her in a cardboard poncho, she does a few clumsy umbrella steps, and King Herod, equally obese, rushes her a gourmet dish, namely the head of John the Baptist. It makes you wonder if the sins Christ was ranting about all had to do with overeating. Are we to believe that Christianity was nothing more than the feeble beginnings of Weight Watchers?"

Claude, his arms tightly wrapped around his chest, his crossed legs encased in tight white jeans, said, "I don't want to discuss the movie."

"I couldn't agree more. To hell with the rotten movie. Admit it was torture, so we can talk about us."

Claude sighed.

"Stop suffering so much," I cried. "It's getting all over the taxi."

A tiny, stubborn, human part of me needed to hear that Claude hated the movie, because, believe me, it's no holiday for a woman of my refined tastes to discover she's living with a fool.

I closed my eyes as the taxi shot across Fourteenth Street, barely scraping past a crosstown bus. The driver reacted the way all cab drivers react when they cross Fourteenth Street, which is as though they've entered the Inferno. He couldn't have been more lost or confused. This was the point at which Claude was struck with the terrible possibility of the meter suddenly doubling. He all but rested his head in the goon's lap, guiding him down Seventh Avenue and into Bleecker Street, as if he were docking the *Queen Mary*. We never got driven to the door, because that meant circling an entire city block. The taxi came to a shuddering halt at the corner of Bleecker and Morton, Claude breathlessly absorbed in calculating a ten per- cent tip. The cabbie grudgingly dropped coins, one by one, into Claude's extended palm, neither of the men considering my prolonged exposure to heat prostration. The transaction completed, Claude went dashing down the street without waiting for me. I scurried after him, already concerned with other matters, such as how I could get to the top floor of our brownstone without being spotted by the psychopath who occupied the ground-floor apartment and spent her days and nights watching for me with murder in her heart.

2

*D*URING my six months of drudgery with Claude, we shared his top-floor apartment in a brownstone on Morton Street. It was a terrific floor-through apartment with two huge rooms, a separate kitchen, beamed ceilings, real plank floors, a skylight, and a fireplace that worked. Talk about the Jewish Conspiracy. I'd like to meet one Frenchman living in anything but splendor anywhere in the world. The lease on the apartment was held by French Television, C.I.A. agents please note.

Claude was supposedly covering news and producing documentaries on the American way of life, for instant viewing in France, in order to make the inhabitants of that cemetery even more smug about their beautifully preserved plots and monuments. Claude's reports were like riot commercials. Student riots, antiwar riots, gay-liberation riots, convention riots, prison riots, ghetto riots; in short, Democracy at work. The only faces he ever filmed were covered with blood or gas masks. His documentaries tore off the masks, so you got the backs of people's heads describing how they became junkies, prostitutes, criminals, old, sick, and crazy. It was a genuine treat to watch one of Claude's specials: rush home, lock all the doors and windows, check out the closets and under the beds, and commence sewing the family jewels into the old fur coat.

To Claude's prejudiced eyes, everything and everyone American was revolting, with the possible exception of migratory workers and Hopi Indians, and you can imagine how they hung around us in droves. This business of Claude being so madly in love with the so-called underprivileged is a joke I'd like to clear up. He made innumerable Communist speeches about injustice and corruption, but when it came down to real life, all he actually cared about were titles and tits. His voice would go hushed and worshipful when he spoke of anyone who came from a family, in quotes, as if the rest of us had emerged fully formed from garbage pails. All these real people from real families were French, naturally, because for some mysterious reason, when it came to Americans, he made no distinctions between inspired intellectuals and the bums blocking their doorways.

I met Claude the freezing February night of Rhoda-Regina's convenient nervous breakdown. Rhoda-Regina is my ex-best friend and current enemy. I had been crashing in her garden apartment following my return to America after five enriching years abroad.

Claude found me huddled on the bottom step of the stoop, after R.-R., in a unique display of American hospitality, had flung all my belongings onto the street. As a matter of fact, I met all my neighbors that famous night, because when a mad woman is screaming and throwing things and is finally bundled off to Bellevue, New Yorkers will gather around and gawk. Only Claude, being a foreigner, offered to help and whisked me up to his top-floor apartment to be a combination concubine-drudge. I have since realized that he hoped I was a victim of rape, or at least a junkie, two of his favorite American specimens.

I went up the stairs behind Claude, tiptoeing like a thief, out of consideration for R.-R., who was long out of the hospital but subject to relapses at the sound of my voice or footsteps. It is ironic how my behavior is determined by the insanity that surrounds me.

We got safely into the apartment, and for a moment I thought we had wandered into the prison laundry as depicted in *The Big House*. The drenching heat had solidified into vapor, and I blindly fumbled for the overhead-light switch. Claude would sooner have seen me dead than leave the air conditioner operating in his absence, which meant that by the time we cooled the oven under the roof, we were both too wasted for it to matter.

"Whew," I gasped, "they've overloaded the boilers. This tub is about to explode. Off with your shoes, man, be ready to abandon ship."

Claude's heavy-lidded eyes were fixed on me in hate and loathing. It was too hot to contend with his temperament. I kicked off my sandals and proceeded to unbutton my sleazy cotton shirtwaist. I walked to the window and pressed Mr. Fedder's magic button. Claude still didn't move. I unhooked my clinging, shapeless bra and dropped it onto the floor.

"Are you planning to stand there all night, Claude? Are you by any chance the new warden in this hole?"

No answer. I headed for the bedroom, where, blinded by droplets of sweat dripping into my eyes, I managed to find my Japanese kimono mixed in with the sheets on the unmade bed. When I came back into the living room, Claude was still standing sentinel at the door.

"Is anything bothering you?"

He responded with an unintelligible mumble.

"Please." I folded my robe over my damp belly and tied the rope sash. "Speak up. I'm not Helen Keller. I can't put my fingers on the radiator and hear what you're saying."

In spite of the heat I felt the slight, familiar stirrings of appetite. I advanced to the kitchen and opened the refrigerator door. The cool air trapped inside felt good, but regardless of weather, opening refrigerator doors makes me happy. My Jewish abductors were insane on the issue of opening refrigerators. If you so much as tried to sneak a look at the pickings, one of them would come running in after you, yelling, "Close that door. All the food will rot." As if you were unsealing King Tut's tomb.

I carried the plate of curly roast beef into the living

room and put it on the round oak table where we did our eating.

"Are you hungry?" The creep still didn't answer. The fact is that Claude, not having been raised by kidnappers, was habituated to regular meals, not scavenging.

"I'm not hungry." It walked! It talked! It went to the kitchen and got itself a can of beer.

"I can't find the opener," he complained, in that same hurt voice I'd been tolerating for two full weeks.

"Why don't you telephone Paul Newman? I read he always wears a can opener around his neck, like a cross. Maybe he'll lend you his."

Claude broke his heart and tore off the aluminum ring on the beer can. He really didn't approve of these modern conveniences. Better for me to do nothing but keep track of his household utensils.

"That movie has certainly put you in a wonderful mood," I told him, twisting my wet hair into a knot and pinning it to my skull. "Remind me not to attend any more public executions with you."

"That's the last movie I'm taking you to."

"I want that in writing."

"You don't enjoy anything but those stupid quiz shows you watch all day."

He came and sat in the captain's chair opposite mine and rested his arm on the oak table. The apartment was furnished very Village Traditional. A bit of Americana, Japanese lampshades, Swedish rugs, Mexican candlesticks, Indian bedspreads, and for color, buckets of sickly avocado plants that Claude accused me of drowning.

I made myself a roast-beef sandwich with one slice

of rye bread and folded the tidbit into my mouth. Claude followed the action as if I were a boa constrictor swallowing a pig.

"If looks could kill," I told him in between chews, "you'd soon find out that yours couldn't."

I adjusted my robe. "So tell me what was so inspiring about that movie? If it was about any other Jewish fag and his mother, would you be so impressed?"

Claude sighed.

"Stop sighing. What terrible thing am I doing to you? I figure we went to a movie, we got home alive, now let's discuss it like two normal human beings."

"You don't need me for that. Why don't you do six normal people discussing it?"

"Is that supposed to mean that you don't feel you're getting equal time in our exchange? Because, if so, I feel obliged to tell you that it seems to me I spend close to one hundred percent of my time asking you what you think about things and getting grunts for answers. Legally, I should be required to apply for a cabaret license in order to live with you. For instance, I'd like to ask you something right now. Why are you looking at me as though red ants are crawling out of my mouth?"

"Don't be disgusting."

"Okay, black ants. And what is this new development that everything I say is nauseating or disgusting?"

Claude's face went soft with suffering. He became the handsome young priest trying to coax the suicidal maniac off the ledge of the thirty-seventh floor.

"You're right, Harriet. I know I'm being hard on you, but that's because there's something I want to talk to you about and I'm finding it difficult."

"Take your time," I said playfully, "just don't take as long as that fag took to die."

"Stop calling him a fag," Claude shouted, his sallow skin suddenly flushed. "You make me sick."

"Thank you," I shouted back, because there's a limit to even the most understanding woman's capacity for abuse.

"I make you sick? Some skinny guy schlepping a hunk of wood that weighs a ton up a steep hill for the express purpose of getting nailed to it, that was beautiful? But I make you sick?"

"We won't discuss the movie," he announced for the millionth time, though it seemed to me he was the one who kept bringing it up. He spread his hands flat on the table and stared at his fingers, waiting no doubt for a larger crowd to gather.

He spoke slowly. "Harriet, we can't go on living together."

"Because of a lousy movie?" I exclaimed in disbelief.

"Forget the movie. The movie is typical. If anything gives me pleasure, you automatically hate it."

"Not true. You're wrong. It's crazy to twist my opinions into personal attacks, Claude. I swear, I genuinely hated it. Excuse me for not being the Marquis de Sade, but my idea of entertainment is not to watch someone bleed to death, even if he is God."

His voice got soft and mean. "Has anyone ever told you what a terrible bore you are?"

"Me a bore?" I laughed, amazed that the rat would resort to such a bizarre accusation. I have since learned never to be amazed at what men will resort to when cornered by a woman's intelligence.

"When you get an idea in your head, when you have an opinion, which is always, you've got to make a speech about it, not once, but ten times. If anyone manages to break in, you bury them; you grind them into little pieces with your big mouth. I've had it, Harriet. I want you out."

"Out? Out where? What are you talking about?" In my alarm I plunged the mustard knife into the heart of the macaroni. "Okay, I get a bit carried away. Maybe I'm too insistent, too eager to communicate. But that just runs in my blood. It's very American to share experiences."

I felt myself babbling to gain time, to find a foothold, because the alarming depths of Claude's anger made me feel like the innocent wife who has stopped to admire a sunset and is about to be pushed off the cliff by her homicidal husband.

"Like hell. You don't communicate. You trample over other people's feelings. You don't even listen to what anyone else says, except to tell them how stupid they are. Anyway, I don't wish to share your experiences any more." His voice was shaking with fury.

"Not true, not true. You're misinterpreting my enthusiasm. It's in my nature to have strong opinions. But your reactions are much more important to me than good sense. For all I know, it was a wonderful movie."

"I am not simply talking about your boring opinions

but about the disgusting way you go berserk when I'm not in total agreement with you. I must like what you like, and hate what you hate, which is everything, or I get no peace. Harriet, this battle between us must end." He slammed his beer can on the table.

I looked at him in stupefied silence, unable to speak, because in order to perform that function, it is necessary to swallow. My protest stayed lodged in my throat. Never, not for one second, had it occurred to me that we were battling.

He took advantage of my physical disability and struck again. "If I presume to like anyone or anything, you go totally out of control. You demand every second of my attention. I am obliged to see nothing, admire nothing, and respond to nothing but you, you and your dazzling insights. I'm sick to death of this aggression that never ends. I want you out."

I found my voice, cracked but usable. "Stop saying that. You'll brainwash yourself. Out where?"

"I don't care. It's not my problem. You have friends, parents, let them help you."

"I told you my parents are dead."

"One day they're dead, the next day they're alive. Harriet, I've made up my mind. I hoped we could spend a pleasant evening, a normal evening, and then calmly discuss the separation."

"Ha," I screamed, as the trusting wife always does when she remembers the preposterous will she signed. "You've planned this all along. That's what you've been doing, brooding out here, night after night, instead of facing me, like a man, in bed."

The full measure of his treachery burst in me like a hurricane.

"Harriet, please be fair."

Fair? How dare men ask you to be fair, before they throw you in the lion pit.

"There weren't even any lions in the picture. They were too damn cheap to throw in a few hungry lions. What about the countless Jews who were consumed by lions? They don't count?"

"You're not going to pull your banana act on me, sweetheart. No matter how nuts you get, we're going to have this settled. I want you out of this apartment. It's my apartment. I took you in because I felt sorry for you. I found you wrecked on the stoop and brought you up here out of kindness. That was supposed to be for one night, remember?"

"Well, how do you think people get together in New York? Were we supposed to be introduced at Tricia Nixon's wedding? Is that what's bothering you?"

"What's bothering me is that six months have passed and you're still here, like a leech, a parasite, destroying my apartment and my life. How long must I pay for a single act of mercy?"

His distortions, the lies he was telling himself and me, filled me with a cold fury, because, as an American, my war against injustice knows no bounds.

"Mercy. So it was mercy that kept me pinned to your mattress until now? What an extraordinary display of mercy. How Christlike of you, Claude. Thanks to seeing your film biography this evening, I suddenly understand it all. But they didn't go far enough. The schmuck who played you only kissed lepers; you, on the other hand, screwed one."

"Stop screaming. It's one in the morning."

"You might have considered the hour before dropping your bomb, my little lamb of peace."

"Enough, Harriet. You made your point. I was not trying to deny that I found you attractive."

"Nonsense. You weren't attracted to me. You were attracted to this corpse you found on your doorstep. You were performing a miracle, not a marathon, don't belittle yourself."

"I said you made your point, but whatever I was doing, you didn't seem to object too much." He had to throw in the self-congratulations, because like all Frenchmen, he thought he had the patent on sex.

"You begged me to stay here while you were breaking the world's all-time mercy record."

"I didn't beg you, ever. This is getting us nowhere. Whatever made me hope you'd be reasonable?" he lamented. "I let you stay here because I was in and out of the city, and it seemed cruel to kick you out. Every time I'd had it up to here," he drew a line on his forehead where his brain should have been, "I had to leave New York, and then I'd come back and foolishly get involved with you, but we always agreed that it was a temporary arrangement, and now it's over, no matter how you exaggerate to serve your peculiar views."

"Peculiar!" I stood up, wishing my wrath could be backed with some solid support, such as a machine gun.

"It's only a word," he said nervously and got up from

25

the conference table, thinking perhaps that in the ten measly seconds it took him to get a beer, I would be packed and out of the apartment. His wish did not come true.

"Well? Do you just go around calling people peculiar? It seems very peculiar to me, and I use the word advisedly, that any time we leave this squalor, be it to see a lousy movie or one of your lousy friends, you become hysterical. It also seems to me that you feel very free to say anything you want about all the dirty Jews who are conspiring you out of being the Dalai Lama of television, but if I make one tiny observation about a movie that had Christ in it, we're having a religious war. Now *that* I call peculiar, and I'd like to ask you if your idea of my role in this household is to be your captive, your echo, your one-woman harem, because if it is, Claude, I warn you, a person such as myself does not transform into an ignorant Arab just for the asking."

"How could I have hoped she'd be sensible?" he muttered.

"You've been doing nothing but hope for the last couple of weeks. Did you perhaps find yourself hoping that I'd be hit by a bus?"

"You won't believe me, but I don't enjoy hurting you."

"But it appears, Prince of Peace, you don't enjoy any of the activities I thought you were enjoying."

"Enough," he yelled and leaped out of his chair. For a dreadful moment I thought he was going to resort to physical violence. I burst into tears.

"Oh, Harriet," he put his hand on my shaking shoulders, "it's not the end of the world, baby. Why are you reacting like this? It's not as if we had planned to be together forever. You know my contract finishes in six months and I go back to France. So it's ending sooner than you expected, that's all."

I reached up and grabbed his arm, clinging to it as though it were the overhanging branch between me and the fatal drop.

"Darling, is that what's bothering you? Are you afraid that in six months we'll be too attached to each other? That it will be too difficult then to make a clean break? Because if so, I assure you, in six months I will wave you off gladly, smilingly, like a happy native seeing the beloved explorer returning to his homeland, laden down with all the loot he can load into his canoe. Believe me, Claude, my object is not to be one of the treasures you steal."

"What are you talking about?" The phony sympathy was out of his voice.

"I won't feel you're abandoning me when you leave me behind to return to your rightful place as head of the Communist Party and possibly even to marry a certified virgin of good family. Immense progress could be made in the next six months. Look at the marvelous changes already." I tried desperately to think of one improvement in Claude, but I needed time to reflect. After all, life is not a quiz show.

He shook his arm free.

"No," he said and began pacing the living room, holding his precious beer can. And then he mumbled, as if to himself, "My friends warned me. I have no one to blame but myself."

"Your friends," I snorted. Because let me tell you all about Claude's wonderful friends, one day when you feel like being sick, all of whom are French and all of whom detest me, because instead of being an heiress, I am just an average American girl.

"So you're letting that pack of snobs brainwash you?"

"How are they brainwashing me? Are they coming up here to tell me that I can't find a clean dish in the filthy kitchen? That the bed hasn't been made since you moved in here? That all my beautiful plants are dead?"

"They are not dead. Stop saying they're dead. Plants are very sensitive to suggestions." I rushed to a hanging window plant and stroked its brown leaves. "You're alive, darling. Don't listen to him. He should be as alive as you are."

But instead of profiting from my sunny disposition, Claude threw up his hands in a parody of Gallic disdain and from between pursed lips muttered, "It's too absurd."

"You're the one who's being absurd, running away from the most authentic, probably the most meaningful relationship you will ever experience, because it wasn't arranged by your mother."

I tried to embrace him, but he paced through my arms as if they were shadows.

"Darling, we have so little time left and so much work to do. You have so much growing, so much expanding before you. How can you cheat yourself to such a rare, such a blessed opportunity, out of some old-fashioned notion of chivalry?"

"You win," he said. I had the chilling impression that whatever I was winning, it was not Claude. He was back at his post near the door.

"With your permission, I'd like to go for a walk and think over all the good you've done for me."

"A walk? Are you crazy? It's a hundred degrees out there."

I could not bear for him to leave the apartment. It's hard to explain how a woman of my potentials found herself in such a position, but at that low point in my life, I suffered a kind of passionate concern for Claude, and I had never felt it more strongly than at the moment the suicidal maniac yanked open the door. We were both engulfed in a repulsive gush of steaming stale air. It emphasized the coolness of the living room. Claude closed the door, as if against a blizzard of pollution, and leaned against it.

"Please, come to bed," I said.

"To bed, with you?" Claude screwed up his classic features as if he were playing games in front of a carnival mirror. "I'd rather sleep on a sewer than sleep with you!"

That business of sleeping on sewers happens to be a French tradition, so I didn't take offense.

"It's very late. We can continue the discussion tomorrow."

"No more discussions, Harriet. Tomorrow is Friday, you'll be out of the apartment by Monday morning."

"Of course," I said gently, "and now to bed."

"Go to bed," he said coldly.

"Not without you."

"I'm telling you for the last time to get to bed."

I obeyed the bully like a punished child. The bedroom was warm and sticky, which was why I fought for the single air conditioner to be in constant action. I threw my kimono on the bentwood rocker and, in the dark, crawled into the desolate bed. I lay there listening to Claude puttering around in the living room. He had been pulling that act night after night, waiting for me to fall asleep. Now I knew what he had been plotting. My body heaved with a childish dry sob. I felt an icy fury wail through me. I wanted Claude to come to me. I ESP'd him to come into the bedroom and need me, but Claude stubbornly brooded in the living room. I lit a Marlboro and disciplined my mind to empty itself of all unpleasant feelings toward Claude. It wasn't easy, but this was not the time to react like a hysterical woman and think in terms of tired clichés, such as rejection. I meticulously reran Claude's frenzied accusations through my total-recall memory. The machine faltered at the word boring and would not play on.

Boring? What boring? It is a fact that Frenchmen find everything except the sound of their own voices boring. If not for an inborn craving for flattery, French ears would have gone the way of fins, tails, and tonsils. Was that a clue? Had I, in my frank American fashion, neglected to lay on the adulation that Claude felt was his birthright?

I felt a wave of gratitude, but toward whom or what escaped me. After the initial blackout, my brain was again functioning. Was Claude out there sulking because he felt cheated of the endless declarations of gratitude that make a Frenchman feel alive? It so happens that gay and outgoing as I am in routine matters, in the privacy of bed, I am your silent, giving, inscrutable mystery guest. I am your bottomless pit of receptivity. Was the poor devil interpreting my modesty as indifference? I would force myself to be more demonstrative. Lucky Claude. Help was on the way.

I killed my last cigarette of the day and must have dozed off almost immediately. As soon as Claude slipped in beside me, I was electrically alert. Dawn was seeping through the burlap drapes.

"What time is it?" I whispered, since I never use blunt conversational tones in bed.

He wasn't divulging classified information. He turned on his side and pretended to drop into a deep sleep. I nestled along his warm back. It stiffened. I blew a breath of soft air on his neck.

"Don't," he said in an agonized whisper.

Since it was already the next day, I decided I had coped enough for one night.

3

*T*HAT NIGHT I had my usual dreamless sleep. I hardly ever dream, which is probably a reflection of the fact that I live my life fully and consciously. I solve my problems while awake and, as a result, spend my sleeping hours resting, not receiving inane messages. My ex-best friend, Rhoda-Regina, who has squandered her last ten years of earnings on analysts, due to her incredible vanity regarding her dreams, used to give me a daily recounting of the marvels she had produced during the night.

How often I would tell her—"Rhoda," I would say, "do yourself a favor. Go to bed with a real man and you won't need to waste your time on nightmares."

Naturally this sensible advice was resented, because Rhoda-Regina expected me to break into rapturous applause and shouts of Bravo, as if each of her dreams rated four stars.

Rhoda-Regina would stagger around her apartment

for hours, stupefied, eyelids glued together, from the dissipation of her private orgy.

Ideally I like to begin my day with a stimulating quiz show. I turned on the set and got Concentration, which is a show that doesn't require brains, but is nevertheless a pleasant warm-up for Sale of the Century, which immediately follows. The drama of my day begins to build as the stakes go up, the questions get tougher, and the opponents confront each other with polite envy and rage.

I couldn't concentrate on Concentration and remembered, as if I had recorded the entire scene, Claude's incredible breakdown of the previous evening.

"Claude," I hollered. "Claude, are you here?"

No answer.

I untangled myself from the mess of crumpled sheets and dived into a bundle of rags piled high on the bentwood rocker. My Japanese kimono, looking more and more like a captured flag, bled and spat upon, was right on the top where I'd placed it. I tied it securely around my hips and went directly to the air conditioner. Sure enough, it wasn't in operation.

"Leave that thing off," an order came floating out of the bathroom. "I don't want to catch cold."

Claude had more theories about the hazards of air conditioning than your vegetarians have about meat. I went into the kitchen, and for a change, there was no lovingly prepared Chemex of fresh-brewed coffee. I filled the kettle and put it on the stove. Another slave day had begun.

I found Claude submerged up to his neck in gray

water. "Get out of here," he said. "I'm taking a bath."

"Well, it's a relief to know I'm not interrupting your baptism. Don't you believe in answering a person?"

"Don't start on me, Harriet. I'm tired."

"You know, seeing you in the tub like that reminds me of a drama I saw on One Step Beyond. It was about this murderer, a doctor, who killed five of his wives before justice caught up with him. The thing that made justice suspicious was that all five of his five wives died in the bathtub, which struck them as too much of a good thing, since the doctor didn't exactly marry paupers. You want to know how he did it?"

"Finish what you're doing and get out of here." Claude pulled himself up in the tub, the black ringlets on his chest straightened by the water. "I want privacy."

"I sympathize. I want the ruby necklace that Onassis gave to Jackie so she'd have something to wear with her ruby earrings, but we take what we get in this life. Right? You want to know how they caught him?"

"No. Hand me the sponge and get out of here."

"There was a time, handsome," I chided him, "when my Arabic prince liked to soak in his marble tub, while his Scheherazade entertained him."

He pretended not to remember.

"There was a time, Royal One, when your faithful captive used to soap her master, and when he was in a benevolent mood, he would invite her into his royal tub. Does he remember that?"

This time he cut off my fond reminiscences by turning the water on full blast.

"This bath is too damn hot."

"Oh, Master, why didn't you let me draw your bath? What else am I here for?"

"Stop being so revolting first thing in the morning. I'm tired."

You didn't have to be Rose Franzblau to observe that Claude found the merest hint of sex disturbing.

"How come you're so tired? Didn't you sleep enough last night?"

"No," came the sour answer. "You kept crawling all over me. I finally gave up and got out of bed. What was that all about?"

"Perhaps it was merely a dream?"

"I didn't shut my eyes. Hand me the sponge, it's at the edge of the sink. Then get out of here."

I arose from my toilette to do my lord's bidding and inadvertently caught my reflection in the medicine-cabinet mirror. I wasn't expecting to greet Sophia Loren, but my God, I wasn't ready for the Bride of Frankenstein. My face looked like it had been crushed into an overstuffed suitcase that Muhammed Ali did me a favor and closed.

"You're destroying me," I cried, throwing the sponge at him. "You should be arrested for what you're doing to me."

"You look the way you always look."

"Lies. Fabrications." I desperately combed the egg foo yong out of my hair. "Are you trying to tell me you invited this face to move in with you?"

Me and my spontaneous nature. I could have auctioned off my tongue to the lowest bidder. That was all

I needed, to remind the crank that I lived with him. Fortunately, Claude was too absorbed in soaping his precious armpits to notice my Freudian slip.

"Your face is still okay, considering the weight you've put on."

To men who are not basically fond of women, every additional ounce of flesh is like a thorn in their side. Fortunately, I had gained a few necessary pounds and was no longer the helpless waif he had captured.

"Excuse me for not being an emaciated wreck any more. Now that I know your tastes run to cadavers, preferably hanging by their thumbs, I'll certainly make the necessary adjustments."

"Don't be so touchy. You still have a groovy figure. You'll have no trouble catching a replacement." He emphasized his sinister statement with a ghastly smile.

"What in the world would I want to replace? Honestly, Claude, the way you talk, you'd think I had nothing on my mind but rape."

He looked embarrassed or bewildered, and concentrated on soaping his legs.

"Would you like me to do that for you, darling?"

"Get raped?"

"No, silly, wash you." I laughed recklessly at that excruciating sample of French wit.

I dried my eyes. "You know, Claude, I may neglect to mention it from time to time, what with the cleaning and cooking and the shopping, I do get distracted, but for a man, you have a wonderful body, and for a Frenchman, it's practically a miracle. Good lord, those runts in Paris, strutting around as if they had something special to show off. It's a blessing how they don't see themselves. But of course, French women are positive geniuses at convincing any gnome that he's Tarzan. I suppose they had to learn the art of flattery in order to assure the propagation of the race. Is your father short?"

"Harriet, I hear the water boiling in the kitchen."

"Oh yes," I jumped up. "Would you like a Nescafé, sweetheart?"

"No. What is this disgusting darling-sweetheart routine?"

"You look like a Greek god."

"Cut it out, Harriet."

I handed him a fluffy towel that I myself had transported to and from the laundromat.

"Let me dry your back?"

"I can manage."

Between you and me, Claude, naked, was a delightful surprise. In his corny French corduroys, fag turtleneck sweaters, and cowboy boots, he looked like any other Russian spy, but undressed, shazam, there appeared a long, lean, compact, subtly muscled runner's body. All his parts, including the sexual ones, were firm and well placed and even attractive. I couldn't avert my eyes from his smooth, strong bulges and curves.

"Stop staring at me."

"I'm not staring, I'm admiring. Honestly, Claude, if you knew how desirable you are, at least to me, you'd stop tormenting yourself about my opinions."

He made a disgusted sound and pushed past me. I followed him into the bedroom.

"Goddamn it, Harriet, quit crowding me."

"Your mastery of English is astounding. Not only your vocabulary, since any dummy can memorize lists of words, but you never even have to think when you talk. It just spouts out. That's what I call learning a language. When you dream about me, is it in English or French?"

"Go get me a cup of coffee. Sugar, no milk."

"Really, you silly. As if I could forget how my favorite customer takes his coffee?"

I went tripping to the kitchen to do my Gunga Din number.

"Here, Sahib." I cheerfully handed him the chipped mug.

Claude eyed the bentwood. "Do I have a clean shirt?"

"Who cares about shirts? What's your big hurry to get dressed?"

"I have to be at the bureau in half an hour."

"Forget your pig career for one minute. You know what I'd like, Claude? I'd like it if we could lie down on the bed, quietly, just relax together and let nature take its course."

I watched his face go scarlet with self-doubt.

"To hell with nature." I quickly revised my scenario. "I'll take nature's course. You just lean back and pretend I'm your harem."

He located an immaculate shirt that my loving hands had tucked into his top drawer.

"This is the last one. Will you remember to take my shirts out today?"

"If I get cancer, darling, I won't forget."

He cleared his frog throat. "And while you're at it, pick up a *Village Voice*."

"That Commie rag?"

"They've got lots of apartment ads. I didn't mean to be so harsh yesterday, baby. Of course I'll help you find something to rent or share, and I'm prepared to help financially. You know my token salary?" he added quickly. "I can't support anyone. But it will be good for you to work like the rest of us peasants." His French cash register of a heart broke into a sickly smile. His loathsome efficiency stunned me, and I found my vocal chords paralyzed.

"I'll be home early tonight," he pulled his shirt over his smooth shoulders and sat down on the bed beside me, "and we'll go through the ads together."

He reached down and found his socks all by his wonderful self.

I grabbed his hand and tried to hinder his progress. It was as though he were putting on armor, not clothes, to protect himself from my touch.

"Aren't you going to give me just one more chance? Are you too afraid to just lie down next to me?"

"Look at that bed," he said evasively, sticking his feet into his boots. "When were the sheets changed?"

"I'll call room service immediately. If you'd stop being so fanatically clean, we could be having a much better time."

"I'm late for work. How often must I repeat myself?"

"So you'll miss one mugging. Isn't saving our relationship more important?"

"I believe I made it clear last night that our relationship, as you persist in calling it, is over."

"But why?" I cried. "Why? Why? You haven't given me one reason why."

"Harriet, don't make a scene. I was very explicit about the reasons."

"Ridiculous. You mean that babble about pots and pans and plants. I'm not a charlady. I'm a sensuous woman. Please, Claude, please. I'm not asking you to take me to rapturous heights. Your feeble efforts mean more to me than all your mountain goats rolled into one. Remember how it was for us at the beginning, Claude? Gigantic. You were a tidal wave. All right. Maybe it's not in you to maintain that hectic pace. I don't care. I'm not like other women. I'm not asking for heaven, Claude, I'm just asking to be held."

When the echo of my shrill voice died out, there was a resounding silence left in the room, as if a monster rock-and-roll concert had ended on one abrupt note.

"Harriet, don't cry."

"Why not? After all we've meant to each other, suddenly you're horrified by my touch."

Claude, completely dressed, took my hand and held it tightly. "I'm sorry if I've given you that impression, Harriet, because it's not correct. I had no right to blame the breakup on you."

"There doesn't have to be a breakup. I don't want to hear about breakups," I wailed.

"You're a beautiful girl, an intelligent girl, a sensitive girl. It's just that we're not suited."

"Are you determined to spend your life with a stupid slut?"

Claude sighed. "I need to be alone."

"What is this suicidal despair? So you haven't been King Farouk for a couple of weeks. It's not such a tragedy."

"Harriet, I'm not a one-woman man. Can you understand that?"

"For most women, yes, but not in my case."

"I must have my freedom. Maybe it's immature of me, but I cannot live with a woman. For me she is a delicacy, a treat, but in my home, no. I suppose I'm a born bachelor."

"All men are born bachelors, but they change. Don't push me away because you fear the change. How many times must I say I don't expect to be dazzled. I don't ask you to be perfect. You'll find me patient, understanding, tolerant, and most important, always waiting to give you a helping hand. And even if you don't change as much as you feel you should change, I love you as you are."

"I have to go to work," Claude mumbled. "I'm late."

"Will you promise to think over what I've said?"

"Will you remember my shirts?" the brute answered. Then he actually slapped his forehead. I dimly hoped he was awakening himself. "Oh, good God, today is Friday, isn't it?"

"I wouldn't know. I'm the laundress, not the court astronomer."

"Charles and his current stewardess are coming here to dinner tonight."

"What? You managed to arrange for that eunuch to come here and gloat over my eviction?"

"Don't be ridiculous. He's been in Washington for ten days. I don't know how to reach him."

Claude went into the living room, which was better designed for pacing.

"When were these disgusting arrangements made?"

"You were there."

"Why does that freak keep inviting himself over when he hates me so much?"

It was too disturbing for me to even think of Charles and the Miss America Contest he paraded before Claude's glazed eyes, in the hope that one of the entries would have the guts to do what he couldn't, namely, to disembowel me.

"He doesn't hate you. He's just a bit frightened of your direct manner."

"Ha," I said, "I forgot, it's not fashionable to hate. It's all fear. Hitler will go down in history as the most frightened man of the twentieth century."

"This is impossible," Claude said, looking at the deep-sea-diving watch that was strapped around his fag wrist. "I'll try somehow to reach him and call it off."

"Couldn't we just not answer the doorbell?"

Claude looked scandalized. I intuitively sensed that it was crucial to my boy friend to keep up appearances, since it was essentially the only thing he could keep up. With that intuition came the wisdom to participate wholeheartedly in his superficial life.

"Really, dear, it won't be so bad. I'll pick up some

cold chickens and cold roast beef and chopped liver and pickled herring. It will be fun. I kid around, but you know I love to entertain your friends."

Claude made a critical survey of the living room.

"No," he said, half to himself, "it's impossible to entertain anyone in here."

"Don't be a goose," I protested. "I'm planning to scrub the place from head to toe. I'll get that kitchen so clean, Charles could perform an abortion in there."

Claude opened the hall door. It was even hotter out in the business world.

"I'll call you later," he said sullenly.

"I promise the place will be spotless. Get plenty of lovely cold white wine," I called down the fetid stairway.

Alone, I turned on the air conditioner. I felt strangely cheered. Due to my eternally optimistic nature, I was already scheming to turn this unwelcome occasion into a triumph. Here was a golden opportunity, call it a challenge, to unveil the depths of my capacity to flatter and charm. I decided to prepare a homemade meat loaf.

*A*s soon as I hit the street, I knew that meat loaf was out. Only a pathological martyr would cook in such weather. The heat sizzled over the filthy streets like an invisible mustard plaster. If you fancy cooked banana peel with pizza and eggshells, there was a feast in the gutter. There were a lot of drunken bums hanging around, competing for nickels with hippies in hairshirts, rehearsing the plague. I dragged myself to Bleecker Street, holding my unmasked breath until I was in the sheltering arms of the A&P. It was freezing in there. I asked a mustachioed clerk where the cold cuts were hidden, but naturally he didn't speak a word of English. "Cold cuts," I shouted into his insane face. He laughed gleefully, as if I had proposed that we both crawl under the check-out counter and knock off a quickie.

I wandered up and down the aisles, pushing this cart that was designed to go backward into my ankles, and

found inspiration in the form of two bright-orange barbecued chickens, a container of cole slaw, plus a quart
of chocolate-chip ice cream, and then, remembering
the French addiction to a procession of courses, a large
jar of pickles, and dinner was served, Madame. The
bill came to twelve dollars, which is my flat rate,
whether I buy a pack of cigarettes or load the cart
with hearts of palm and Nova Scotia. I paid the tariff
and went sloshing in and out of the dog puddles, back
up Morton Street. I wish to say one word about dogs
in New York and then forever hold my peace, which is
that they should turn on their fag boy friends and bite
off the proudest part of their fag anatomies.

I had hardly ripped off my dainties when the doorbell rang. Could it be that my swarthy admirer had followed me home? I looked through the peephole and
beheld the jangling presence of my best friend, Maxine.

"Wait," I yelled, because I'm very modest in front of
the hostile scrutiny of women. I slipped into my silk kimono and opened the door.

"Harriet." Her burglar alarm went off. "I'm so glad
you're home. I'm expiring from the heat. You look fantastic!"

I must admit that she did, too. I checked the hall to
see if a drooling convoy of tourists were snapping at
her heels. There was a sufficiency of rhinestones in her
thong platforms to refinance the purchase of Manhattan.

"Come in quick," I said. "How do you have the guts
to walk around in public like that?" Maxine, Jewish

mother and wife, was fighting off an airtight pair of white shantung hip huggers. Above that carnage, through the transparency of a fishnet polo shirt, you could see a kosher delicatessen.

"Oh, really." She switched to a throaty laugh. Maxine had more accents than Peter Ustinov, but unless you punched her in the stomach, you never heard the real one. "I just came from my hatha-yoga class. It was madness in this heat. But you know, for an Indian it's chilly out there. My teacher was so pleased with me today. He said I had the spine of a five-year-old, but I'm completely worn out."

She dropped her retarded spine into the wicker armchair, her stubby legs clearing the floor.

"My lips shrivel up in the heat." I watched as she applied yet another layer of lip gloss to lips greased thick enough to cause a major oil slick along the Atlantic coastline.

"You're lucky to have such a wonderful skin," she crooned, but since she didn't look up from her gold compact, I couldn't tell which of us was supposed to be so lucky. She glanced up. "Not a wrinkle or a blemish. What do you use?"

"Sperm," I said, damned if I'd let her drag me into one of her beauty commercials that begin with compliments and finish with her imploring me to consider plastic surgery.

"You're terrible." She giggled and fell back into her valise. She emerged holding up a small pink package. "I bought you the most fabulous moisturizer, guaranteed to banish those black pouches under your eyes in less than three weeks."

"How long are you planning to visit me?" I asked. "I have a lot of things to do."

"Just till I cool off," she said and put a pack of king-size Kools on the coffee table. She lit a cigarette with an efficient click of her gold Dupont lighter, her tiny, pointy fingers rigid with wedding bands. She was the most adorably married woman in the Western Hemisphere.

Maxine was under the impression that since we had jumped rope together in Brooklyn, our insults were predicated on love. The real reasons that Maxine insisted on continuing to know me were one: to feel fortunate that instead of being me, she was her wonderful, eleven-room, married self, and two: in order to hear sex stories about Claude, since the mere mention of his uncircumcized name made her hysterical. To guarantee herself these pleasures, she harped on our historical and emotional bonds.

"How are your parents?" Maxine never failed to ask.

"Alive," I said, in an attempt to cut that boring ritual to the bone.

Anyway, it was all the information I had. Gorgeous George and his trainer had retired from the ring and weren't giving out any interviews from their camp in Los Angeles. Whenever I called them, be it six in the morning or ten at night, or four in the afternoon, my call interrupted their napping tournament.

"Hello Ma," I'd say, after letting the phone ring a

few dozen times, "this is your daughter Harriet." Why turn a long-distance call into a quiz show?

"Harriet?" I could feel her struggling to surface.

"How are you, Ma?"

"Fine, fine, the weather is beautiful here. I was just taking a little nap."

"How is Dad?"

"Should I wake him?" she'd worry me. "He didn't sleep a wink all night. I know, because he kept me up."

"Just say hello for me."

"Oh," she'd groan, sinking back into dreamland, "he'll be heartbroken that he missed your call."

"Do they like California?" Maxine politely pursued the inquisition, her rosy face contorted with sincerity.

"What do you want from me? What do they know, like, don't like? When they're not sleeping, they're sitting in a kitchen a real-estate agent told them is located in California. If they went in for liking, they'd sign a suicide pact."

"You talk that way," said the uncanny Jewish mind reader, "but I know you miss them."

"I miss them," I informed her, "like I miss having the clap."

Maxine registered shock. From the day she had climbed the top of the mountain and married a Professional Man, our mutual parents had magically transformed into sacred beings. Forget the twenty-year poker hustle conducted around her mother's formica dinette table. Forget everything that didn't jive with being a periodontist's wife. One of the major deletions

I was asked to make in my memory bank was the entertaining fact that Maxine had been the neighborhood nymphomaniac. From the age of four on, she would put out for a half-eaten Tootsie Roll. As she matured into adult promiscuity, she waltzed a troop of sexual freaks through my parents' parlor, since the gambling casino she called home wasn't exactly suited for secret love trysts. Only marriage had liberated her from sex. Her debt to society was paid. Now, her past must be forgotten, her file pulled, her record wiped clean. I saw her the day she returned from her honeymoon, bursting with charge accounts.

"It's silly." She giggled girlishly. "My Jerry is so jealous, he gets crazy if I look at a man." That no doubt meant she could detect breathing.

"Well, you can hardly blame him," I said judiciously. "It's probably a guy you blew in your youth."

"Me, are you suggesting that I fooled around with boys?"

My candor caused Maxine to drop me for three refreshing years. It was only when I'd returned from Europe and Maxine had packed eight years under her chastity belt that she felt a charitable impulse to resume our friendship. This impulse did not include the friendship of Dr. Jerry. I had to be satisfied with photographs of him modeling the latest sporting equipment. From the pictorial evidence, she had turned him into a chicken-fat hemophiliac. My impression was, if he nicked himself shaving, out the stuff would gush, till you were left with a non-recyclable plastic container.

He was not, to put it mildly, the star you would cast in your TV series about this swinging dentist who caps Loretta Young's teeth.

"How is Jerry?" I asked and immediately suspected that Maxine had hypnotized me into mouthing these inane words.

Was she ready to tell me!

"He's wonderful, he's so wonderful. I just don't deserve such a wonderful husband. It should only happen to you, Harriet, it's all I wish. Guess what he gave me for my Norton's birthday?" My Norton was their six-year-old deviated septum.

I was mad for her guessing game.

"A hysterectomy?" I guessed. But for a change she wasn't paying attention. Her eyes had wandered off to her walk-in closets.

"Guess again."

"A vaginal orgasm?" I tried gamely.

"Really." She heard me that time and smartly flicked an ash with her ringed finger.

"A dark-brown, twelve-inch vibrator?" I was beginning to enjoy the challenge.

"Is sex all you ever think about? He built me a sauna in the dressing room," she said flatly, sensing that I wasn't going to fall on the floor in paroxysms of joy.

She waited for a response, but when it became apparent that I'd sunk into a wide-eyed coma, she upped the ante.

"And he's engaged Felicia Bernstein's masseuse to do me every morning at nine."

"Hmmm," I said, "if anyone came here at nine in the

morning, they'd arrest Claude for practicing unnatural acts."

She sucked in her breath. My friend had what she coyly referred to as a crush on Claude. Since he wasn't a Jewish husband, she knew it was only my cunning and vigilance that kept him from jumping on top of her and violating her ears off. She eyed the closed bedroom door as if she expected to see a thick ooze seep out from under it.

Maxine had this heartbreaking problem, which she had confided to me during one of our intimate girlish chats. Her problem was that producing Norton had almost destroyed her, and there wasn't one contraceptive method on the market that suited her unique system. The Pill? Was I perchance suggesting suicide? It gave her migraine headaches that transfixed the medical profession. Diaphragms shot out of her every time she hit the jackpot, which was always, and her profuse body fluids did likewise to any precautions Jerry employed. The mention of coils caused her to hemorrhage like a tsar, but as she discreetly put it, Jerry was an angel of understanding. Apparently the final solution for this tragically fertile woman was to have her sex life in her head, and Jerry, I presume, conducted his in his patients' bleeding gums.

She interrupted my ruminations by asking if she might impose on me for a glass of water. While I was in the kitchen, she added ice to her modest order. She came to watch me fight the ice-cube tray, which was welded into the freezer like King Arthur's sword.

"Jerry bought me the most marvelous new refrigerator," she remarked absently. "It manufactures darling little ice cubes and drops them into a plastic bucket."

"Bring it around with you the next time you barge in." I handed her a dripping glass. She held it as though the wetness was pure slime. In between delicate sips she told me her latest troubles.

"It's such a bore. I'm on this diet and I have to drink eight to ten glasses of water a day. I feel like I'm going to explode, but I must lose ten pounds by next Friday, and it's supposed to work like magic. You should try it, Harriet. Ten pounds less would be very becoming on you. Of course, you don't have my pressures and social obligations to be attractive. If Claude likes you the way you are, I guess you're set for a while. But me, it's one invitation after another. Next week it's Lenny. You know, if not for Jerry, Lenny wouldn't have a tooth in his head. So he's been begging us to save him one weekend on his yacht. And you know Lenny, he's constantly surrounded by the beautiful people, black and white, I'm delighted to say, just so long as they're famous. God knows the competition I'll run into on Lenny's yacht, and I have absolutely nothing to wear, nothing that fits, except what you see on my back. How are things with Claude?" she finished, so I shouldn't get the impression that she was self-absorbed.

"Terrific," I said, "if your ambition in life is to be a one-woman bordello."

"It's terrible, isn't it?" Her eyes flickered around the messy room. "It's all they think about. My Jerry is driving me up the wall."

Her Jerry, the Phantom Stud of Central Park West.

"Of course, it's really all you have to do. But me, there are servants to manage, dinner parties to arrange, Norton, my *au-pair* girl, my analyst, my yoga, group therapy, and now a masseuse."

I welcomed her commiserations. "You're right. My life with Claude is one uninterrupted bout of carnality."

Maxine understood. She set her water glass on the coffee table and circled her loving-cup lips with her hands.

"He has so little time left to be with you, it probably weighs on his mind. How much longer does he have in America?" The head of immigration couldn't have been more concerned.

"Hopefully, Maxine, you'll be out of here before he has to leave. Isn't it time for you to get back and clean Jerry's tools?"

She looked at her gold watch, which was set in a gold band surrounded by gold bracelets.

"Just a few more minutes. I want to stop off and see Regina when she gets home. Did you two make up yet?"

"Who's that?" I demanded, because of all her hypocritical roles, the one I despised most was Maxine as peacemaker. She rushed back and forth between me and Rhoda-Regina, reporting to each of us how sick the other one was. When she came to visit our tenement from her estate on Central Park West, she did a full Queen Elizabeth touring a Ugandan hospital.

"Now don't be that way." She smiled her Mrs. Periodontist smile.

"If you are referring to my ex-friend Rhoda, no, we haven't made up. And I wish to remind you that after twenty-five years of calling somebody Rhoda, I find it extremely difficult to switch to Regina."

"If it makes her happy, what does it cost you?" Maxine recited in a chillingly accurate imitation of my mother.

"And when she decides she's Van Johnson? Will you be ready for that one?"

Maxine glowed, already having a splendid time at the expense of my nervous system.

"She's greatly improved. She's sculpting again. She got her job back at Greenwich House, and she and Sidney seem very adjusted." I was astounded to find myself listening to a diagnosis of R.-R.'s condition.

"Wonderful," I said. "Is she still tipping the scales at a neat two hundred?"

"She's not fat, Harriet. She's just very large-boned," the contented midget decreed. "Anyway, I really think that if you apologized to her, explained what you thought you were doing, she'd be only too glad to forgive you. After all, you don't just throw a lifetime friendship out the window."

"She did," I said grimly, "and I don't wish to discuss it. If she's too sick to realize that I had her best interests at heart, I don't want her friendship."

"You're not being fair." Maxine's perfectly round, bright brown eyes were pools of Jewish wisdom. "It could affect anyone's mental stability to wake up from a deep sleep and find a black stranger sharing her bed." The great liberal now called all of them, including writers, senators, singers, and the doorman, black.

We had had this discussion at least one thousand times, but Maxine, whose mind was as matured as her spine, couldn't hear it often enough. A look of sublime bliss settled on her moon face. I did not intend to run through the routine again. A person had to live with Rhoda-Regina's twitches, her spasms, her asthma, her blinking, her stuttering, before understanding why, on a mission of mercy, I had miraculously produced a man to appease her torment.

"I'm sorry I couldn't get Marcello Mastroianni, but he was busy knocking up Catherine Deneuve that night."

"But she was fast asleep."

"Rhoda awake is unfuckable, and if that's all you have left on your agenda to talk about, I can survive your leaving."

Maxine lit another cigarette with a neat click of her 18-carat gold lighter.

"We won't talk about it," she promptly agreed. "But I just want to say one word. I think you're being unfair to Regina. The fact is, she took you in when you were flat broke, you had nowhere to live; you forget, but you were a breathing skeleton when you got back to America. She acted like a true friend."

It occurred to me that if I smeared lip gloss all over Maxine's squat, soft body, I could probably force it down the incinerator.

"I agree," I said bitterly. "She certainly was a better friend than you, who never gives anything but lip service."

"If you saw the stack of unpaid bills Jerry has on his desk this minute, you'd understand why we can't possibly hand out money."

"Have you come here to scrounge a couple of dollars out of me?"

That shut her up, but only momentarily.

"It's impossible to have a conversation with you."

"You're doing okay," I reminded her. "And now, if you don't mind, I'm having guests for dinner."

Maxine, who was the laziest practitioner of yoga in the West, didn't move from her perch on the wicker armchair. I left her and went into the kitchen to unload the groceries. Only her piercing contralto followed me.

"The thing you won't believe is that Rhoda-Regina is not your enemy. Far from it, she's worried about you. We've discussed how you lay, day after day, flat on the mattress in her studio, either too exhausted or too afraid to go out. She thinks that something awful happened to you in Europe, and I do, too. But you're so sensitive and angry, I'm afraid you'll jump down my throat if I ask you."

I came back into the living room and took one of her Kools.

"What happened in France?" Maxine leaned forward eagerly.

"I found out I wasn't French."

"No, no, something happened to make you come home this way. Was it a man?"

"Maxine, you know I had mononucleosis."

Maxine dismissed the disease with her well-married

hand. "My doctor says mononucleosis is psychological."

"If you're working into your psychiatrist spiel, I'm going to call the police and have you thrown out of here."

"You see," she said triumphantly. "You won't listen. Harriet, I'm your oldest and probably only friend. You can't go on this way. You must go to a doctor. I'd send you to mine, but to be honest, I don't want to share him. It's very possessive and childish of me, I know; we've been working on it for months."

"You have my promise, I won't steal him away from you."

"But, Harriet, your behavior isn't normal. You're so furious all the time, so rude, so disagreeable. I've known you all my life, and I forgive you. But I swear, I don't know how Claude stands for it. This place always looks like a cyclone hit it."

"I can live without him, too."

"Something is wrong between you and Claude." She pounced on the possibility with all the eagerness of Dr. Barnard finding a beating heart in a battered donor.

It occurred to me that one of the worst aspects of the breakup would be the free pleasure it would give Maxine. If I could at least charge her admission.

"Harriet, Harriet," she wailed, "you must go for help. You can't go on this way, alienating friends, lovers, your family, everyone. A woman can't survive in this society completely isolated, alone, unloved. And the basis of it all, of all your problems, is that you don't love yourself. It's so clear. Just look at how you're neglecting yourself. It breaks my heart. It's all self-hate.

How can anyone love you if you don't love yourself? Fix yourself up."

She gave me a quick once-over and launched into her cosmetic view of the universe.

"Streak your hair a little; some highlights up front would brighten that muddy look of yours. Get a manicure. Lose some weight. Buy a few decent clothes. It's a pity you're so tall or I'd give you my old things. My girl walks around looking like a million bucks. Make yourself attractive so Claude can be proud to be seen with you. It's not too late. All relationships go through their difficult periods. You wouldn't believe me if I told you some of the insurmountable obstacles Jerry and I have conquered, because we were willing, because we worked at it together."

Imagine my surprise to find myself listening attentively to Maxine's abuse.

The bitch picked up the scent of my attention. "Is it another woman?" she demanded breathlessly. If she had had a tail at the end of her stunted spine, it would have pointed straight up into the air. Would that my life was the mindless soap opera Maxine yearned to hear.

"Could you manage not to be a fool for five seconds a day?"

"Well," she demanded, "what's happening between you and Claude? Isn't he planning to marry you and take you back to Paris with him?"

If there's one thing on this earth that irritates me, it's when a dumpy, frigid, former nymphomaniac assumes that my tongue is hanging out, thirsting for marital bliss. It goes without saying that though ideally suited and ecstatically happy, Jerry and Maxine had flown directly from their wedding ceremony to group therapy, paying top prices for the privilege of insulting each other in front of an audience.

"I'll make you a promise, Maxine, and then let's adjourn this summit conference. I promise you that the day I decide to marry anyone I hate as much as you hate Jerry, one: you'll be the first to know, and two: I'll seek professional help."

Did Maxine get the message and leave me in peace? Not a chance. She sat there radiant with superior knowledge. "My dear, that is precisely your sickness. You think everybody hates their life. You're wrong. I don't hate Jerry. I love him. My heart may not palpitate when he walks into the room, but I'm happy with him. I appreciate his devotion and goodness. I love our child, our home."

"Excuse me very much, but if it's love, sweet love, that makes you parade the streets like a crazed drag queen, if it's happiness that drives you to come sniffing around here like a starved alley cat, give me hate and misery."

Hurrah. I was heard. I wasn't speaking in a dead tongue. Maxine heaved herself upright, sucking in her stomach, and performed a full *grande dame* on me.

"You're hopeless, you and your defenses. You're even sicker than I feared. You remind me of a girl in group we had to throw out. If anyone touched on the truth, she turned into a howling cornered animal."

"So that's what we're having. A sample group-therapy session. I thought we were taping for the Johnny Carson Show. Leave. Go quick, tell Rhoda how hopeless I am before you forget one word of this interview."

Maxine proceeded silently to repack the tons of crap that had exuded from her vinyl satchel. I might have had the small but gratifying satisfaction of delivering the last word, but Lady Luck is obviously being paid handsomely to ignore my existence. The phone rang, and it would have required a deadly karate blow to the jugular to get rid of the intruder.

It was Claude, sounding as though he was reporting in to his parole officer.

"Harriet?"

"Claude darling, I've been waiting for your call."

Maxine went into a full Marcel Marceau extravaganza so I should say hello for her.

"The plans for tonight have changed," he told me.

"Oh, rats, I've been cooking and cleaning and shopping like a field hand all day. Well, darling, we'll have a nice quiet dinner alone."

"Will you let me finish what I was saying?" he snapped.

"I'm all ears, sweetheart."

"I was able to reach Charles, and we've arranged to have an early dinner at La Bonne Femme."

"Oh, no," I said, because my loathing for uptown fag restaurants is practically a phobia.

"Harriet, I was thinking it would be better if I have dinner alone with them and get home early."

If not for the hostile spy sitting in my living room, I could have been very explicit about my objections.

Maxine took a metal teasing comb out of her valise and messed up her streaked mop of hair to look as though a battalion of mercenaries had had a go at her and one Turk more or less wouldn't faze her.

"Nonsense," I said gaily, "I'd love to join you."

There was a very long pause from the other end of the wire.

"Hello, Claude?"

"I'm still here."

"Wonderful."

"I think it would be better if you didn't come to-night."

"Darling, I'll be at the Bonne Femme with bells on, I promise you."

"Oh, Christ. Will you behave yourself with Charles and his girl friend?"

"I'm dying to meet her. I wouldn't miss it for the world. What time did you say?"

There was another monstrous pause. Maxine was leaning forward in her chair, her flexible spine no doubt tingling.

"Seven," he said finally. "But if you make any trouble . . ."

"Isn't that the place where they serve that fabulous cheese platter with all those broken crackers?"

This time there was no confusion about the silence, because he slammed the receiver down.

Since there was now no need to go into my scrub-lady routine, I flopped down on the couch and lit a Marlboro.

I could tell, from the expression on her face, that

Maxine had elected to forgive me. Let it never be said that pride got in the way of her pleasure.

"Ugh," I said, "could Jerry shoot some Novocain into my gums and freeze my face into a smile for tonight?"

"Why didn't you give Claude my regards?" my sit-in pouted.

"For crying out loud, Maxine, could you please stop thinking about yourself for one second?" I myself was already struggling with the issue of what to wear. Entertaining at home, I would have been sublime in bare feet and a saffron Burmese prayer robe, but to appear before a pack of hostile faggots would have given pause to Cinderella's godmother.

"What's wrong between you and Claude?"

I couldn't answer because quite incredibly tears of exasperation filled my eyes and throat. My guest levitated off the wicker chair and landed beside me.

"Harriet, tell me. Let me help you. I see you're suffering."

"Please, Maxine, get the hell out of here."

"He wants to throw you out," she announced with hideous precision. "You're going to be back in the same mess as when he picked you up. Harriet, Harriet," she moaned, and it passed through my mind that of all the countless treacheries my mother had perpetrated, naming me Harriet was the most infamous.

"I can't stand by and let you ruin your life like this. You can't waste any more years on these affairs. You're almost thirty. What's going to happen to you?"

It came then, the fleeting nightmare of me, old and

gray, dispensing paper towels in Bloomingdale's rest room.

"It's not as if you were me, born to be a wife and mother, or even Regina. She's an artist, a teacher. She can take care of herself. But you? What can you do? What do you want? You have to want something in this life."

"I want you to stop torturing me, Maxine, and go home."

"I'm your friend, Harriet. I beg of you." She clasped her hands together, and if not for her Jewish knockers protruding at me, I might have mistaken her for Deborah Kerr.

"Please, go to an analyst, a clinic, a group, get help before it's too late, before you've ruined your chances for having something permanent, something real. A woman needs security. A home, a place. I don't say you have to get married, though I know you'd marry Claude in a second if he asked, but it has to come from somewhere or you're ruined."

"Me marry Claude? Are you insane?" I shrieked. "Marriage is all you and Claude think about."

"Don't try to tell me he's asked you to marry him, my dear. He knows your story. He knows you've been passed around from man to man, and he'll just pass you along. Why should he worry about you when you don't worry about yourself? Claude will get married one day, but not to you. He'll find a respectable girl and have a respectable home. Believe me, I know what Claude wants."

I for one had had enough of her disgusting jealousy.

"Maxine, I'm sick and tired of you hanging around here drooling over Claude. I didn't force you to marry that nauseating piece of blubber you keep complaining about. If you're unhappy, divorce him, but I advise you not to do so on Claude's account. If I was not so pathologically incapable of hurting people, I'd tell you exactly what Claude thinks of you, the artificial respiration I've had to apply after you've smothered him in your mountainous boobs. Many's the time I've had to remind him that you're my friend and I expect him to be courteous to you. Now I see I was wrong, because your fantasies are eating away at the little sense you were born with."

It was rewarding to see the demented vivacity go out of Maxine's fat face. It reminded me of Joan Fontaine when Rochester takes her up to the tower to meet his maniac wife. Maxine pulled herself upright on her rhinestone platforms, but she refused to be offended. She persisted in forgiving me. I suspected that if I commenced to hammer a nail into her head, that look of toleration would stay smeared all over her understanding face.

"I only hope you find out what you're missing before it's too late."

"Thanks. I only hope you don't, or you'll go up on your roof and become the first topless mass murderer of Central Park West."

She then made me a fabulous promise. "I'll call you as soon as I get back from Lenny's yacht and tell you all about it."

"Who the hell is this Lenny you keep harping about?"

Before closing the door on her bursting hip-huggers, I spotted the bright-pink package of moisturizer that the jealous harridan had left on the coffee table. I scooped it up, ran into the hall, and heaved the vial of venom after the descending pygmy.

5

*A*FTER THAT stimulating invasion of privacy, you can imagine how eager I was to join Claude and his gang for dinner. In spite of knowing that the only thrill in Maxine's life was to have a heart-to-heart chat that left her victim prostrate, gasping for breath, I had, out of courtesy, allowed her in, so now she could march straight down to Rhoda-Regina's apartment and continue having a perfect afternoon. It felt as though I could press my ear against the floorboards and hear Maxine relieve R.-R.'s suffering by informing her of my impending rift with Claude. Why was Rhoda-Regina suffering? A good question, and the only answer I've ever arrived at is that she was suffering because she could not stop comparing herself with normal people. I had warned her.

"Rhoda," I said, "don't torture yourself with comparisons. Five years in Europe have completely transformed me, while you, except for the addition of a few pounds, are exactly the same Boy Scout."

I always kidded Rhoda, because when we first met, at the tender age of six or seven, residing as we did in semidetached villas in Brooklyn, she wore only boy's clothes. That came about because she had three older brothers and her father was a tailor. The rest was just plain Jewish common sense. What were they supposed to do with the pants when the youngest son outgrew them? Make stuffed derma? It's true that in our childish ways, we all poked good-natured fun at Rhoda-Regina, but from the way she carried on with her ten uninterrupted years of analysis, you'd think if not for those outfits she would currently be the widow of Aristotle Onassis. That she had also inherited her father's musculature never occurred to her as an obstacle to feminine perfection. And furthermore, if the ideal female automatically lived in a Zelda Fitzgerald paradise, why wasn't my life one delirious fandango? However, she couldn't spare one second from her incessant brooding to reflect on anyone else's destiny. No matter how normal or relaxed she seemed, all you had to do was wink at her and say, "Clothes make the man," and you had a volcanic eruption on your hands. Rhoda-Regina had been my oldest and best friend. I'd known her almost as long as I'd known myself. We'd gone through school together, except that she, being insecure as a female, had gone on to collecting degrees. We'd sailed to Europe together, me to stay for five crucial years, during which I'd grown out of my Brooklyn chrysalis into a creature of indeterminate origins, while

Rhoda-Regina had barely lasted through the summer, rushing back to her beloved highway-robber analyst like Dracula making dawn tracks to his coffin.

A word to the wise. If you happen to be an American citizen, born and bred, and you come upon hard times abroad, go directly to the Ethiopian Embassy. I kid you not. When I appealed to the American Consul for help, he hustled me on a plane to New York so fast I had no time to say goodbye to my great love, Mac-Donald. For all he knows, I'm still in the American Hospital recuperating from a bout of mononucleosis. The thugs were taking no chances with letting a free spirit slip through their black-leather gloves. They even kept my passport, which is no doubt currently in the possession of Mrs. Martin Bormann.

Once officialdom had finished with me, there was no one to turn to but Rhoda-Regina. My adoptive parents had moved their act to Los Angeles; Elizabeth and Richard were incommunicado on their yacht; Jackie and Ari were feuding again; Maxine hung up on me. Desperate, I dragged myself to R.-R.'s door and rang her bell. I tried to conceal how shocked I was at Rhoda-Regina's enlarged appearance. R.-R. looked like a massive version of the Statue of Liberty after some vandals had knocked the torch out of her hand.

"Surprise," I said, "it's me, Harriet."

"Harriet?" the sleepwalker mumbled. In a certain unselfish sense, I had arrived in the nick of time.

"I would have written," I explained, "but it turned out I could get here faster than a letter. Ha, ha. Aren't you going to invite me in?"

With that discreet hello, my Calvary began. At first Rhoda-Regina was genuinely grateful for my company, but it soon became clear to me that she wanted all the advantages of my stimulating personality with none of the inevitable dues. After all, when two individuals live together, regardless of sex, they must consider the differences in taste, or those two persons will begin to feel like a Calcutta family of fifteen packed into a drainage pipe. It was as if Rhoda was refusing to acknowledge my corporeal existence. I am not a genie. I do not vanish into a bottle upon solving my master's problems. Just because I happen to have uncanny insight does not mean that I am other than a flesh-and-blood woman with normal appetites. I admit right now, a confession to all the world, I need a place to sleep, a quiet, private place, not a mattress in some crank's studio. I never could communicate this simple truth to Rhoda-Regina. For a one hundred percent revolutionary, which she claims to be, defender of women's rights, black rights, prisoners' rights, Puerto Rican, gay, and Vietnamese rights, when it came to my rights, the good old capitalist line was drawn. In short, Rhoda-Regina refused to give up the bedroom, the only logical division of space, since she expected me to remove myself from her studio whenever she felt the slightest urge to create more of those ridiculous plastic torsos. I am not a machine. I am not an automaton. I cannot be turned on and off. Excuse me. I'm only human. I'm affected by my physical and mental state.

I admit I needed a great deal of sleep upon my return to America. It also happened, due to five years spent in another time zone, plus jet lag, which is an established scientific fact, that I slept at unpredictable hours. Shoot me, or, better yet, give me the bedroom and ignore me.

It was not as though she needed her bedroom for romantic purposes. Never. You could conclude, as R.-R.'s houseguest, that the entire white male population had been wiped out by infectious hepatitis.

Rhoda's so-called sculpture made sleeping in the studio a wide-eyed nightmare of being laid to rest in a communal grave. As I may have mentioned, she called herself an artist. Why not? Old maid was never anyone's most flattering self-image. Being a Boy Scout, she couldn't simply call herself an artist. Oh, no, she felt obligated to make things in order to merit the title. What she made were these plastic body fragments. Thumbs five feet tall. Lips you could walk through. Ears you could swim in, and then, tipping the other side of the scale, full figures four inches tall, legs you could wear on a thin gold chain, microscopic hands you could sit on the head of a pin. These plastic amputations filled the room, because needless to say, crowds were not rushing to her door to snatch up her productions. You didn't exactly have to be Sigmund Freud to figure out her size fixation. A person of Rhoda-Regina's proportions must have fluctuated between feeling she was a captive in the land of pygmies or a giant who could hang us all from her charm bracelet. How often I used to tell her, "Rhoda, stop brooding about your size. Having a perfect figure may be a blessing, but believe me, it's not the only thing in life. A saint may come along who is not primarily concerned with proportions, but when he does, if you drag him in here, be prepared to administer mouth-to-mouth resuscitation."

That great liberal wanted me awake, alert, available, job hunting, shopping, cleaning at all times, except—important exception—at mealtimes. Then, she wished me dead. From the way she carried on, you would think that throwing an extra cup of water in the soup was going to make Rhoda-Regina a pauper. Truly it hurts me to make petty accusations. Mine is a large, a generous nature, and it's therefore not like me to notice how base practically everyone is. My God, you would think we were lost in a lifeboat from the way she rationed the food. As a defender of women's rights, she consistently boasted that she hated to cook. I, being practically European, love to cook, but not when I'm expected to rub two potatoes together and produce a banquet. Furthermore, everything they say about two women in a kitchen is true, which may be, women's lib or no women's lib, why all great chefs are men.

So Rhoda did the cooking, and the shopping, since I'm no mind reader, and she would invariably try to squeeze a week's dinner out of a barely adequate two-course meal. Since my sleeping habits were, by her standards, irregular, it follows that my eating habits were equally reprehensible. I admit right now, let me volunteer the information, I am not one of Pavlov's dogs. I get hungry when I get hungry, not when someone rings a bell at me. True, I'll eat just to be sociable, but acute low blood sugar is another matter. I dared to need nourishment when, according to Rhoda-Regina's lights, I should have been out demonstrating, marching, protesting, anything, but not eating.

Rhoda-Regina returned late one evening from her teaching sinecure, a cushy little setup where, for thirty-eight dollars of taxpayers' money per day, she imparts to minority children the mysteries of the plastic ear lobe, information which undoubtedly propels them directly out of the ghetto into public office.

She headed straight for the refrigerator like a dog obeying a supersonic whistle. At first I thought she was having an apoplectic fit because I hadn't found the time to wash the bowl; inmates were expected to keep their utensils clean. It gradually dawned on me that she was flipping over a modest snack I had downed to combat protein starvation.

"You have to be kidding, Rhoda," I defended myself. I was reluctant to antagonize her, but just because someone is putting you up for a couple of days is no reason to become her whipping boy. I have learned the hard way when it's appropriate to apologize. If it ever comes to pass that my behavior inconveniences anyone, I will be the first to say sorry, but I refuse to go around excusing myself for exercising normal functions. I include stemming severe malnutrition among the norms.

"Have you no consideration at all?" She nestled the empty bowl against her broad, flat chest. "Couldn't you leave a piece of the pot roast for me?"

Now I employed what might seem a very strange, even dishonest tactic to anyone who was not looking into Rhoda-Regina's severe eyes. I said, "What pot roast?"

She gasped and loosened her grip on the bowl, causing me at first to believe she had broken it, until I identified the blood smeared over the front of her white crocheted shawl as good old American ketchup. Rhoda-Regina favored ponchos, shawls, capes, and bulky peon skirts, Communist disguises which she foolishly imagined minimized her bulk.

"The pot roast that was in this bowl, pig." Rhoda-Regina was someone who couldn't afford, cosmetically speaking, to get angry. Her coloring went from cooked to raw, and her round, brown, doggie eyes, under heavy black brows, shriveled into burned meatballs.

Rhoda-Regina looked down at her stained shawl. "Ketchup." The word hissed out of her cooked head. "Where the hell did ketchup come from?" Needless to say, it came from the Heinz factory, but I didn't think she was in the mood for lighthearted banter.

"Oh, of course," I solved the mystery, "Sidney drowns everything in ketchup."

"Sidney?" Her face resumed a more normal color, for her, that is. I had snapped the spine of her seizure.

"He came by to see you this afternoon." I continued to administer the successful treatment.

She smelled a rat. "Sidney knows I work Tuesdays." Oh, God, that madly jealous mind of hers was busy thinking the worst. In solving one crisis I had created another. As if I would touch that black pudding with a ten-foot fork. It never occurs to these absurdly competitive females that it is the prerogative of a highly desirable sex object to pick and choose.

"Please, Rhoda," I said, "control that suspicious mind of your. I have no designs on Sidney, regardless of what he may feel for me."

"Sidney wasn't here," the desperate thing insisted. "You just made that up. You ate the pot roast."

"Who ate the pot roast," I sang, "a new musical review by the Muslim Minstrels."

Need I observe, Miss Stonehenge didn't crack a smile. Sidney! Only Rhoda-Regina could get unhinged over that black imitation of a rape fantasy. Some hot relationship they had. Sidney would saunter over in his ridiculous black-leather get-up which, I suppose, was intended to shriek sex symbol but made me think deep-sea diver. You practically had to assist the leather mummy in and out of chairs so he could go creaking to the bathroom. As I said to Rhoda-Regina, "Thank God, he doesn't wear the headgear or we'd need a derrick."

Those two immovable objects would curl up in front of the fireplace in my quarters, forcing me, from my thin pallet, to participate in their tender romance. On those nights Rhoda-Regina was quite willing to relocate me in the precious bedroom, but no thanks. I am not a pawn on a chessboard.

Until the wee hours of the morning, the two injustice collectors would snuggle up to each other, comparing the trials and tribulations of being a misfit. They actually convinced each other that a change in government would make them more desirable. Comes that revolution, please seal me in a vacant cement bunker.

"Listen," I called from my mattress one night, "I couldn't help but overhear your political debate, and frankly, if you want my opinion . . ."

"We don't," the lady of the team grunted. But Sidney, who rarely had the opportunity to converse with a white woman of my caliber, shut her up.

"Nonsense, Regina," he said, in a silky voice that, if you happened to hear it over the radio, would conjure up images of a suave playboy assisting you into his Rolls-Royce.

"Let's have your frank opinion, Harriet." Sidney told you your name every time he spoke to you, a little nicety he picked up from a mail-order charm school. Because of a nail, as they say, and that was the first nail in my and Rhoda-Regina's domestic casket.

Never taking his fascinated eyes off my charismatic being, Sidney lit Rhoda's cigarette. Paul Henreid was alive and well in a black body on Morton Street.

"Go on, Harriet." His voice caressed me. Rhoda-Regina inhaled fiercely.

"Well, when I was living abroad, the relationship between men and women in Rome, in London, Paris, wherever, and you'll be happy to hear it didn't matter to anyone if the man was black or white, the women, however, tended to be white. After all," I laughed in a conspiratorial let's-ignore-Rhoda-Regina fashion, "if black men were satisfied with black women, they'd have stayed home, which certainly wasn't Paris, but the point I was making is foreign men don't feel castrated if a foreign woman happens to know the time of day. Except some of those imported black men, present company excluded. Thank God, I didn't have them to deal with, because I'm not and never have been a dumb blonde. But me and the other women, the ones not looking for a black bruiser to do them in, and you'd be thrilled at how many of those there are. Offhand, give or take a few, I'd concede the entire female population of Sweden and Germany. Anyway, the normal women didn't try to achieve with demonstrations what we could demonstrate in bed, if you get what I mean. In a culture, however, such as the one we're having our discussion in, where sexual differences do not lead to sexual intercourse, which is the general rule in Europe, you of course come to resent not only color distinctions, which are after all a proven fact, but sexual distinctions as well, which in my frank opinion are a blessing."

Sidney's rapt attention, his Oriental slanted eyes fixed on me, his dark, well-shaped hands gently stroking his Othello-cropped beard made me lose track of my argument.

"What was I saying?" I pleasantly interrupted myself. Fortunately, I wasn't on a stage where I had to keep performing, even if it meant making up some gibberish.

"Oh, I think you said it." Sidney's white teeth glistened in his dark face.

If I were a sex-starved masochist, he might have made a conquest. That, dear friends, was the extent of my passionate affair with Sidney. Please go try to convince my jealous girl friend, Rhoda-Regina. The truth is, he and I hardly ever exchanged another word. For all I know, his conspicuous avoidance of me made R.-R. suspicious, since Rhoda was no slouch at ferreting out reasons to be miserable.

Back to the famous conflagration. "Goddamn it," Rhoda exploded, "get your filthy body off that mattress. You lie there like a slug all day and all night. The only time you move is when you crawl into the kitchen and devour every crumb of food in the house. Am I your servant? Your cook? Who the hell do you think you are, lying there like an invalid, complaining, constantly complaining about the service, the disturbances? You're driving me out of my mind, do you hear? My analyst says if I don't throw you out, she won't continue treating me. But I won't throw you out. I'll kill you instead." (Note: It was veritably impossible for Rhoda-Regina to get through a normal discussion without at least one reference to her supposedly infallible analyst, into whose mouth she usually put thoughts and words that sounded emphatically Rhoda-Regina to me. It was as if by tacking "my analyst" over her trivial opinions, they were given the Good Housekeeping Seal of Approval.)

I felt a small shock, a *frisson* as we say in Paris, when she delivered the extraordinary quote about throwing me out. I knew I was dealing with a disturbed person, but disturbed or not disturbed, until she murdered me and was removed from the bosom of society, the apartment was her private stockade. To enter it was to become subject to her order. No matter how many of her threats I repeated to the local police, until I could deliver my mangled body as proof positive that she was criminally insane, she was entitled to her legal rights.

Crazy but not stupid, Rhoda-Regina knew this and gave full vent to her moods. The honeymoon was over. It was time for some serious reappraisal.

"You're ruining my life. I hate to come home from work. I can't invite my friends over without you slandering them. You're costing me a fortune. No matter how much food I buy, it's all gone the next morning. You never express the smallest gratitude, never a thank you, never an offer to help."

It was like being trapped in a room with one of those crazies you frequently see parading down the streets of New York, having loud abusive arguments with themselves. Why hadn't I realized how sick she was? Why hadn't I understood the significance of those insane layers of shawls? Poor Rhoda-Regina. What a destitute fate awaited her. I am not a doctor. I don't carry a hypodermic of tranquilizers. Therefore, I was obliged to wait out her seizure.

I just lay there, my arms crossed over my breasts. A dead queen at final rest in her sarcophagus. Wouldn't you know it? As if I wasn't coping with enough of Rhoda-Regina's problems, there, under my still fingers, big as a pineapple, was an unfamiliar growth. It was too early to know if it was malignant or not. My arms and legs liquefied and the ceiling swam dizzily before my eyes. That was all I needed, my left breast hacked off. My perfect symmetry destroyed. No. If it was malignant, I would beg the surgeons to cut off the oxygen. But would they? Could they let a young and beautiful girl die on the operating table? Butchers that doctors are, they still have families to face.

"When are you getting the hell out of here?" Her distant voice filtered through the blood pounding in my ears.

"As soon as there's an available bed in a city hospital," I replied.

"What are you talking about?"

"I didn't want to tell you, to worry you, before we were sure. Now, I'm sure. Rhoda, I have cancer."

There was a shocked and welcome silence in the room, and then Rhoda-Regina, who was not entirely devoid of human feelings, emitted a long, low, animal wail and rushed out of the apartment.

Alone at last, I forced my disciplined mind to ignore the cancer and concentrate on Rhoda-Regina's madness. What was destroying her mind? Could I help her? Was I not delivered to Rhoda-Regina's door for some purpose? A deeper voice, a cosmic voice, if you will permit me, whispered in my ear.

"Help Rhoda."

Easier said than done. Where should I start tackling that mammoth job? I meditated. I emptied my overwrought mind as if I were an usher emptying a packed house. I was soon rewarded. Up from the deep trenches of my unconscious floated an insight. The insight was that Rhoda-Regina had never experienced your average sexual bliss. She was waiting for me to take her by the hand and lead her into the real world. She would never receive the attention and help she needed from her woman's liberation cover. The only sexual attitude they had liberated her to express was a deep, abiding resentment that she couldn't join the teamsters' union. Had I been insensitive when I told her, "Rhoda, I have nothing per se against your karate classes, but rather than pin all your hopes on a rapist, wouldn't a cruise make more sense?"

Yes, I ruthlessly accused myself. I had been insensitive. Whatever shabby benefit Rhoda drew from the other klutzes in her consciousness-raising group was automatically forfeited when she came home to face me. Clearly I had not achieved my enviable consciousness in a roomful of shrieking malcontents but in the arms of the ultimate taskmaster, an insatiable man.

Just as I was dozing off, the solution came over the public-address system, perfect in its simplicity. Find Rhoda-Regina a lover. Thanks a lot, but where? He'd really have to have an exceptional sense of humor or dedication to take on Mountain Girl. How without Howard Hughes's checkbook at my disposal could I locate such a rare specimen and then bribe him into Rhoda-Regina's clutches? Not easy once he'd seen the Iron Maiden clump across the floor. But experience had taught me that the problem sighted means the solution is near. I would find a way. Lucky Rhoda. I should have such a friend.

The rest of my stay with Rhoda-Regina are the dry bones of history. Why dig them up? Suffice it to say she was beyond help. I suffered the classic fate of the Good Samaritan. A vow: if ever I run across Rhoda-Regina lying in the gutter bleeding to death, I'll carefully step over her broken body and keep on my way. Leave her to heaven, as they say. After all, would I have answered the ad if I had imagined for one second that it meant Bellevue for Rhoda-Regina? I may not be a saint, being an exceptionally earthy woman, but would I intentionally torment Rhoda-Regina, as the lunatic insisted, while tossing my personal effects out the studio window? When I found him, the ideal foreigner, stating his qualifications in one of R.-R.'s precious Communist newspapers, a political bonus I hadn't hoped for, I offered up hosannas. The advertisement read:

> Soul brother, exceptionally endowed, desires sisters, in singles or teams, size, color, age no obstacle; well-versed in French and Greek; photo on request. Write Box 7961.

Forget the photos, number 7961. The position is yours. Everything was falling into place, which I have often found to be the case when I am in touch with my inscrutable powers.

I answered the applicant by return post, racing against the endless refrain of R.-R.'s, "I want you out of here today." I stalled her with wild tales of a parental check en route from the wastelands of Los Angeles; I pondered aloud whether I should selfishly buy one-way passage back to Paris and my true love, MacDonald, or if my duties lay in the opposite direction, with the culturally and spiritually impoverished golden children of the West. The prospect of great distances opening between us momentarily stunned the beast, and I hypnotized her with speculations about my imminent departure, till I had Rhoda mindless and purring in front of our humble fire. I won't detour here to describe how stingily the miser rationed the logs, as if we were holed up in the Arctic awaiting the spring thaw. If not for my genuine squirrel greatcoat, Rhoda-Regina would have returned from work one fine day to be greeted by my stiff corpse. I lived, slept, and ate in my coat, which may have been her miserable game, to spare herself the painful confrontation of my innate and modest grace. Between the freezing temperatures, ostensibly maintained to protect her plastic monstrosities, and the scraps of food I was expected to feed on, she managed to keep me immobilized on the mattress, barely alive in my fur-lined grave.

Mine is not a vengeful nature. It would never occur to me to empty all the garbage pails on Morton Street outside Rhoda-Regina's recently barred ground-floor window, any more than I would dream of sending an anonymous letter to the Immigration Department regarding the un-American orgies prevalent in Claude's illegally occupied apartment. Let bygones be bygones is my motto. I try, wherever possible, to give my persecutors the benefit of the doubt. But this particular escapade of Rhoda-Regina's, her twisted reaction to my feeble but well-intended efforts to relieve her pitiful frustration would make your leading glutton for punishment bow out. I learned my lesson. If people are determined to be crazy and unhappy and you don't have it in you to ignore their silent cries of pain, if you happen not to be a Zen Buddhist, whose idea of fun is some posture freak burning himself to a cinder without slouching, get out of the line of fire. The incident itself hardly matters. I now realize that Rhoda-Regina was searching for any excuse to vent her rage at me. I could do no right. The mere fact that I was witness to her wretched existence made me the hated enemy. Like all misshapen people, she had what I call the leper complex.

Since it was apparent to me, if not to her, that no normal man would have the guts, no less the stomach, to crawl into her bed, my idea was to lure him to her side by the psychological ploy known as mystery. Believe me, if not for the brilliant discovery of veils, tents, and ankle bracelets, there would be no Arab population. Number 7961, tantalized by the unknown, would be slipped into Rhoda-Regina's service without the time-consuming formalities of small talk. After all, the object of the players was not mental compatibility.

In my letter to 7961 I suggested we meet in the studio on R.-R.'s consciousness-raising night on the town. There would be plenty of time when he arrived to explain about Rhoda-Regina's rape fantasies, her puritanical preference for the sneak attack, her baby-elephant wish to be overwhelmed. Like all great strategies, my plan was simple. Since Rhoda-Regina had taken to avoiding me, I could count on her going directly to her bedroom. Her well-primed seducer could wait with me in the studio till all was quiet. Then he would slip silent as a dream into Rhoda-Regina's arms. It was perfect. Even I, after five years of repeated liberation in Paris, felt a small twinge of excitement at Rhoda's prospects.

Agreed, he didn't turn out to be Sidney Poitier, or, for that matter, Rhoda's Sidney, but soul he was by any standard. The fact is when I heard his timid knock at the appointed hour and eagerly flung open the door, I couldn't at first locate him, what with the gloomy hall being a mugger's paradise. He was a small, shriveled raisin of a man, and whether he knew Greek I cannot say, but his French was nonexistent and his English equally bizarre. He was in no way the individual you'd compose from your fantasy photo file, but was Rhoda-Regina turning down movie contracts? It was not an easy matter to explain the setup to Lloyd. I believe his name was Lloyd. I never established if that was his name or the self-effacing manner in which he said hello. Details. He cringed at the word rape, so I discarded psychological insights. The truth is he never seemed to comprehend my plan, but the little octopus was as cooperative as he was dense and willingly drank my red domestic wine while listening to this buildup I gave to Rhoda-Regina that her own mother wouldn't recognize.

Of course, I experienced some nagging doubts, but doesn't reality always introduce doubts? My imagination had conjured up a dashing Lloyd, but was the real thing any reason to disappoint Rhoda-Regina? Why assume in some adolescent fashion that we had identical tastes? After all, did we agree on anything? Finally, what did R.-R. have to lose? A crippling inferiority complex? A petrified libido? Wasn't Rhoda-Regina depriving herself of the stuff of which memories are made, and what, if not memories, is it that distinguishes man from the common housefly? I almost felt, and I'm not one of your syndicated bleeding hearts, that I was offering my tragic hostess that most precious of all gifts, a past, ripped as it were from my abundant storehouse. Nothing was sadder than to contemplate a senile Rhoda-Regina looking back with cataracted eyeballs at a life devoid of love. I chose to be optimistic. If there was a crime, that was my crime. I refused to take the coward's way out, to concede the hopelessness of Rhoda-Regina's condition. Ask me what I think of her chances now that I've regained my objectivity.

If you had heard the piercing screams emitted by that madwoman, and the running, and the knives flashing, you'd think she'd never before seen a naked man. Fair is fair, Lloyd was exceptionally endowed. So much so, you'd expect his endowment to tip over his little brown body. But even a blind person could have seen that he was the frightened party. He scooped up his clothes and was out of the window, and gone in one dazzling leap. Jesse Owens could have taken lessons from him. I tried, but discovered, and I offer my experience gratis to potential suicides, that it takes considerable practice to hurtle out of a window. If that is your preferred method, start training immediately by tying a rope between two ordinary kitchen chairs.

I rushed to the door, but Miss Psycho seemed to be everywhere, blocking all exits. All the warnings about fat people being light on their feet came home to roost.

Enough. Why bother with excruciating details? What should have been Rhoda-Regina's deliverance deteriorated into a farce, a drawing-room comedy, amusing only if your idea of theater is a public hanging. The fracas must have sounded like a swinging party, because two officers eventually showed up. One was black and the other white, which radicals will no doubt be gratified to hear, but both equally indolent. They shuffled around the apartment, pretending to take notes, as Rhoda-Regina performed her dervish dance, complete with war whoops and lunges at me.

"Arrest her, stop her," I shouted, as my squirrel greatcoat went sailing out the window.

"Name of occupant." The white one roused himself from his stupor, his ball-point pen poised over his notebook, his face concentrated and serious as that of a child tracing the alphabet.

"Lizzie Borden, what difference does it make?" I screamed. "That's my genuine fur coat!"

"You two live here together?"

I sensed the direction of his filthy criminal mind. "No," I protested. "Certainly not. I'm just here to help her."

"Did she call you? Did she mention if she'd taken anything?"

Sex and drugs, it was obviously all they knew, so I decided then and there not to fight City Hall.

"God knows what she took. Your guess is as good as mine. If you saw the characters who crawl in and out of this place . . ." But my desperate attempt to enlist their sympathy in Rhoda-Regina's plight was literally choked short by the destructive cow herself. Fingers heavy as stone landed on my neck, and Rhoda-Regina squeezed with all her demented might. Only then did the cops relinquish their journalistic ambitions and go to work.

"She's on a bad trip," one of them finally summed up the situation.

They threw a striped bedspread over Rhoda-Regina's squirming body and pulled her off me. I followed them out to the squad car. Huddled at the curb, looking frightened and forlorn, was my faithful coat. I quickly rescued it, ignoring my other treasures, scattered about like the charred remains of a plane crash. I was too depressed and shocked by my ordeal to care about my possessions, each one a unique souvenir of my travels.

None of the drooling jackals hanging around the fringes of the scene cared to plunder while the police showed so much interest in me. I volunteered Rhoda-Regina's name, but when they invited me to accompany them to Bellevue, I declined, pointing significantly at my worldly goods.

They got into the car and slammed the door. The black cop winked at me. "It's a great life if you don't weaken." I swear I wanted to elope with him, but leave it to the destructive so-called helpless types like R.-R. to end up snug and warm in firm masculine custody. She was lying in the back of the car, content and motionless under her striped shroud. I felt a twinge of envy as they whisked her away, leaving me to a growing circle of fans. My knees were shaking, so I sat on the bottom step of the cold, wet stoop. The groupies moved in, fascinated but too shy to request my autograph.

"Is anything the matter? Can I help you?" Those were the first words addressed to me by the French rat who at that point in my career was simply the foreign face on the top floor. If not for his French accent, which had such civilized connotations, I would never have rewarded him with a small smile. It pains me to reflect how those two exploiters benefited from my upheaval. Claude, in ways too obvious to list, and Rhoda-Regina, by achieving her goal, which was to get me out and Sidney in. Yes, in one Machiavellian stroke she accomplished it all. Her scheme became crystal clear to me when she reappeared in Sidney's protective embrace.

When will some enterprising reporter from *The Village Voice* stop bragging about his sex life for one second to investigate the ins and outs of Bellevue's observation racket? Just why are the crazies promptly released? Do the doctors perhaps share in a weekly pool, a lottery, based on the number of murders their discharges will commit? At any rate, Rhoda-Regina returned to her ground-floor apartment and took her menacing post behind the bamboo blind, watching with murder in her heart for the one false move that would land me in her homicidal clutches. Small wonder my relationship with Claude faltered. How could I concentrate on his bloodsucking demands when three floors below my *bête noire* waited?

6

I DIDN'T have to consult my astrologer to know that I was having one of those days better spent in a closet. My morning with Claude was sufficient evidence that my stars were in collision, but on top of that, to suffer through Maxine's invasion and then to find myself reminiscing about Rhoda-Regina's ingratitude, while ahead of me loomed a dinner with Charles and his latest party girl, felt more like the end of the world than a mere personal tragedy.

How can I describe a human being as malicious and irrelevant as Charles? He was that most superficial of all specimens, a French playboy. His life was devoted to the pursuit of amusement, a dedication made somewhat difficult by a lack of interest in anything that couldn't be injected or swallowed in tablet form. As heir to a French pharmaceutical fortune, he was spending his life swallowing the profits and, of course, courting amusement.

"Amuse me," he would dare you, vacant-eyed, stuffed to the gills with drugs. I would find myself babbling about the population explosion or the impending California earthquake. "Boring," he would roar triumphantly. "You're boring me!" At the moment, he was alleviating his boredom by parading battalions of bunnies, starlets, gymnasts, debutantes, and go-go dancers for Claude's inspection, in the hopes that my boy friend would latch on to one of his protégées and crate me off to the Bronx Zoo.

What is the proper attire in which to dine with your enemies? I dug through my wardrobe, piled high on the bentwood rocker, in search of an appropriate answer. My heart began to beat out this refrain about having nothing to wear. I opted for the mismatched effect, currently so fashionable yet ideally suited to my unconventional looks. At the bottom of the bentwood body count, I rescued a long, cotton, tie-dyed skirt that can go absolutely anywhere. I chose to complement it with, of all inspirations, a sheer green Mexican overblouse. The color combination created a meeting of nature, and not just your everyday placid meeting but nature in convulsion.

I had barely four hours in which to transform myself from a hausfrau to an exotic creature of the night, but I hadn't had a convalescent mother for nothing. We had our shortcuts. I slipped into my fineries, got under the shower, and in one fastidious burst of energy shampooed my hair and clothes. I hung my costume over the shower rod to drip dry. Next, just in case the dinner party traveled to our living room, I cleared out all the crud. By then, it was time to work on my face.

As I mentioned, I don't have what you would call conventional good looks. However, with a translucent makeup base smoothed over my pale skin, my large expressive eyes outlined in kohl, and my dark shag framing my exotic cheekbones, you'd wonder what Egyptian tomb had been pilfered.

I was ready by six o'clock and stood in front of the mirror wondering if what I saw corresponded to my intentions. The tom-toming of my heart introduced a few doubts. To assure my composure, I prescribed one of Claude's dynamite French tranquilizers. I put the others in my shoulder bag, just to be on the safe side. Rather than risk an international incident, I banked the air conditioner and finally crept noiselessly down the sweltering staircase, carrying my thong sandals, particularly anxious to spare Rhoda-Regina the anguish of seeing me so resplendent.

The humidity in the street must have been a thousand, and I staggered to Sheridan Square in search of a taxi. I was lucky to stop the first cab I hailed, because not being Maxine, I was not thrilled at the attention I was receiving.

I told the cab driver where to take me and leaned back, well served by the tranquilizers. Relaxation was not part of the ride. Oh, no, the driver had other plans. This one was your Uncle Bernie, who should have been the president of Yale, but as a victim of the quota system found himself hacking. He longed to share his worldliness with me.

"I bet a lot of people have told you, you look like Anne Bancroft," he said, gazing into his crystal ball.

"Why? Has she been complaining to you lately?"

We drove in silence, but only till we were caught in crosstown traffic. He then presumed to share his military expertise with me. "Oy, the crime, the terrible crime of genocide we're committing. It's splitting the country in two, like Germany was split in two for what they did to the Jews."

I sensed an unwelcome note of familiarity. "Listen, Bernie," I informed him, "I happen not to be Jewish and therefore have no objections to the Vietnamese war or any other war, past or present."

After that I was able to smoke my cigarette in peace.

I tipped him in a fashion that would erase the smallest suspicion of my being Jewish, and head held high, I entered the restaurant.

Charles and his date were standing at the crowded bar. There was no sign of my boy friend.

"Where's Claude?" I asked, going up to them, searching Charles's junkie eyes to see if he had received the good news yet.

"He just called. He'll be a bit late." Charles shook my hand.

"Did a swell assassination turn up?"

"Ah, Harriet." He laughed. "Always so deliciously amusing and always so beautiful."

Yes, I thought, the rat has told him about the old heave-ho.

I couldn't help but notice an icy blond lady clinging to his elbow. She had what is called a golden helmet of hair, sleek and neat, curving along the line of her slender jaw. She was dressed in a gleaming white, silk-jersey halter and yards of pleated white silk pants that managed to cling to her slim hips and legs. Charles, the faggot, was also immaculate in a white linen mod suit and white boots. I stood there beside the white medical team, feeling like a collision victim who has been rushed into the emergency unit.

"Harriet, I'd like you to meet Baba," Charles proudly announced, his glazed eyes pretending to be focused.

"What was that name?" I addressed myself to him, because as yet there was no shred of evidence that she wasn't a deaf-mute.

"Baba," she supplied, in my favorite flat, nasal, hick twang.

"Baba?"

"My real name is Barbara." Icy blue eyes fringed with dark blue lashes. "But when I was born, my baby brother couldn't pronounce it and the name Baba just stuck." Her teeth were as brilliantly white as her uniform.

God, I demanded, what are you doing to me? Stop this torture, you Miserable Creep. Since Claude hadn't arrived, I could delay my charm tactics for a few minutes.

"If you don't mind, I can manage Barbara," I assured her. It was like taking candy from a hooded cobra.

"Charles," she whimpered, pronouncing the "ch" like the first two letters in Sheldon, "don't they have our table yet?"

"I'll find out," he said, snapping to attention. What a marvelous whip these little white marshmallows crack.

"I hate to stand at bars, don't you?" she confided in me, elaborately unaware of the men ogling her.

"Not if I have a drink." Everyone got very alarmed and active about taking my order, and I was obliged to keep them waiting while choices raced through my brain.

"Why don't you have what we're having?" Charles suggested, which seemed an easy way out. I was soon handed an ice-cold martini. It was just what I needed; in fact, it tasted like bitter but welcome medicine. I was balancing my second martini when Claude came sashaying into the bar.

He acknowledged me like I was the crawling green slime and held on to Baba's hand with a pause that said now his entire slob life would take on significance. I could tell that she was attracted to him. The way I could tell was that she completely ignored me and Charles and pleaded with shyly enamored eyes for Claude to rip off her clothes and throw her on the floor. Charles's pimp face beamed approval.

A waiter, inconspicuous in a bright-red cutaway, led us to our table, dropped cement napkins into our laps, and handed us gigantic menus designed for a race of glandular freaks. Rather than stand on my chair in order to open the unmanageable billboard, I turned to Charles and said, "Well, Charles, what do you suggest we send back tonight?"

Charles, the unamused, who could barely digest a cup of warm water, was renowned for the number of dishes he found inedible. Claude glared at me, and then he and Baba vanished behind their menus, doing God knows what. I held up my empty martini glass to one of the cadets hovering around our table.

"I think you've had enough, Harriet."

"Enough what?" I demanded, and then to Baba, who was a study of brilliant white confusion, "My boy friend is so impossible. He watches me like a hawk. Claude, darling," I winked at him, "why don't you order four dozen oysters?"

My martini arrived, and I paid no further attention to the usual French crisis about what was fit to eat.

"Oh, dear," Baba mourned, "everything looks so delicious, and I simply must lose weight."

"Where?" Claude protested, as though someone had accused him of spitting on the marble floor.

"Everywhere," she directed him, just in case he had overlooked one inch of her perfection. "I have to stay below a certain weight to keep flying."

"That's right, you're a stewardess, aren't you?"

"Airline hostess," she corrected me. My, my, who would have thought we'd hit it off so well?

"Gee whiz, it must be hard work, waitressing up there with everyone throwing up and crashing and everything."

"Harriet!" I heard a distant masculine command.

"There's something I've always wanted to ask a stewardess, I hope you won't mind my asking you, but you're the first stewardess that I've met socially. Maybe I've flown with you, even been served by you, but who looks that closely at the Rockettes? Tell me, do you believe that stewardesses and nurses are pathologically promiscuous as a result of their occupations constantly confronting them with death?"

I have an uncanny knack for drawing out new acquaintances by making them feel importantly informed.

"Well, I really don't know." She played with her smoked salmon. "Next time you land in a hospital, why don't you ask one of your nurses?"

How the French pigs laughed at her witticism.

"Last week," she droned on, rotten with power, "Charlton Heston was on Flight 602 to Rome with a private nurse."

"I bet you meet lots of famous people," Claude said, admiring her, as you might admire Mrs. Martin Luther King.

"Gangs," she agreed. "Once I had Dr. De Bakey on Flight 809, coming out of Dallas. It made me shudder to look at him. I think transplants are so against human nature, like a dreadful science-fiction movie come true, and all the terrible questions about whether the person is legally or physically dead. I don't approve of it," the blond philosopher declared.

I recall strongly advocating transplants. "The heart is a machine, a pump, a mindless, soulless, gutless pump. What difference does it make whose pump is pumping you? Do you really give a damn what pumps you, Barbara?"

I held Claude's eyes in snakelike communion.

Charles came out of his nod. "The smoked salmon is atrociously salty."

"I had Edward G. Robinson on Flight 706, out of Africa, immediately after his heart attack," said the heart authority, "and I know, from the way he spoke and acted, that he didn't want any heart but the one he was born with."

"Where are you from originally? You have such a charming accent." My lover steadied his head by cupping it in his hand.

"You won't have heard of it. Webland, Nebraska," she said, with the hideous vanity of hicks.

"That's silly, of course Claude's heard of Nebraska, haven't you, sweetheart?"

Baba did an imitation of Claude, cupping her chin in her palm and giving me her undivided attention.

"Has anyone ever told you that you look just like Barbra Streisand?"

"No."

"I once had her on Flight 47, coming out of Vegas, and really, you're the spitting image."

"I'm a foot taller than she is, and my nose is a foot shorter."

"Not so much her actual looks . . ."

"I'm not Jewish, if that's what you're insinuating. But Lauren Bacall, Rex Harrison, Piper Laurie, Claudette Colbert, Natalie Wood, Charles Boyer, Tony Curtis, Dinah Shore, Sammy Davis, Paulette Goddard, Kirk Douglas, Paul Newman, Laurence Harvey are." I had a list of Jews as long as your arm.

"Not Rex Harrison," she wailed. The rest I was welcome to.

"I had him on Flight 912, coming out of Heathrow, and he bought champagne for all of us."

"Tough, honey, that was Jewish champagne you guzzled."

A waiter came over and whispered something to Claude. He communicated a message to me, about lowering my voice.

"Is this a reform school or a lousy restaurant?" I was far too entranced with my new friend to worry about my public image.

Charles awoke from another refreshing cat nap and decided to break in on our intensely exciting meeting. "Have you ever been in an accident or a near accident?"

"Only once. It was terrible. Omar Sharif was on the flight. He was returning from a bridge tournament. It was rather thrilling, the way he kept chanting Moslem prayers. But I've decided, it's ridiculous to be scared of crashing. You can't go through life afraid of the unforeseeable. If your number is up, you go, even if you're sitting home watching television."

It was astonishing the amount of knowledge packed into that frozen blond head.

"That's easy for you to say, but when you've lost both your parents in a plane crash, you'll sing another tune."

I poured the rest of the wine, dregs and all, into my empty glass.

Baba shriveled up in her chair. I hoped that Claude had noticed the transformation. Take her out of those fancy white pleats, get her into a hoover apron, and she'd scream Appalachia.

"Harriet, what the hell are you talking about?"

"You know what I'm talking about. I'm talking about character, and compassion, and commitment. I'm talking about frigid blond whores . . ."

I suddenly found myself seated on the floor, surrounded by concerned faces peering down at me.

"Get her coffee. Maybe if she had black coffee? Last month Stewart Granger got bombed on Flight 804, coming out of London, and we sobered him up in no time."

"I'm not Stewart Granger, I'm not bombed, I simply fell off the chair. I lost my balance. If it can happen to the Flying Wallendas, it can happen to me. No one accused them of being drunk. I'm sick and tired of your filthy lies."

"Get her up, can you lift her up? You take one arm, I'll take the other."

A waiter rushed over to throw a tablecloth over my corpse. "Can I help?" he breathlessly asked.

"This is a family affair, sir. My mother here and my father and brother are trying to cheat me out of my inheritance by signing me into a so-called nursing home that has a cemetery camouflaged as a baseball field."

I fainted when I realized I couldn't walk or stand. My poor crippled legs.

I came to in the back of Charles's Mercedes. The outrageous dyke had my head in her lap and was pawing me.

I sat up. "So it's me you were after, sly pussy." I tried to kiss her on the lips and ended up sucking on hair spray. "Ugh, Miss Black Sheep, I have something to put in your suggestion box."

I came to for the second time, feeling precisely like Mrs. Skeffington when she regains consciousness and is informed that due to a bad bout of scarlet fever, she's gone bald. It felt as though I didn't have any skin, or whatever it is that keeps the body in such a tidy package. I was a puddle, a carcass decaying in a black room, in a soundless room. It occurred to me that I was dead and buried, and waiting at last to confront Super Creep. I pushed against the lid of the coffin, and my hand met no resistance. Only dark, thin air, so I considered the possibility that I was in my bed, in which case why was I alone, and just where was my paramour?

"Claude," I whispered, patting the sheets and pillows, "Claude, where are you?" Unless he had magically transformed himself into a book of matches stuck to my ass, he was definitely not in the bed. I sat up, and the earth jolted on its axis. When my feet touched the floor, the quake began. Clearly, I had to get out of the room before the ceiling collapsed. I struggled with the doorknob and broke out of the bedroom, dizzy from the effort. I leaned against the wall, caught my breath, and perceived in the distance the welcome glow of a faint light. Like any lost animal, I headed for the light. Imagine my relief to discover that I was not alone. There in the comforting halo of light was a strange misshapen beast. The sole survivors of earthquakes can't exactly pick their company. I crawled closer to the fantastic mound, which I knew was alive because I could hear it breathing. You will never guess what I found in the cesspool of light. There, stretched helplessly on his back, was Claude, and seated on his flat lap, pinning him in an unbreakable hold, was none other than sister Baba.

She was stuck to him, bobbing up and down like a coconut drifting on choppy waters. As I got closer, I could actually hear a sucking, slapping sound. If you closed your eyes and blew out your brains, you could imagine that you were in a boat and the sound was made by a gentle sea lapping against the side of the vessel. But then, unless some unfortunate passenger was drowning, how could you ignore a moaning, groaning repetitive wail? You could say it was the wind or a distant motor. I couldn't.

I strained my open eyes, and a curious phenomenon occurred. The room turned red. I saw a red lamp on the red floor draped with a red scarf. I saw the silhouette of a red couch and a red coffee table. I saw Claude's busy red hands rubbing Baba's naked red behind, his legs, her thighs, his chest, her breasts, red, everything red, as though the world had been dipped in blood.

"Yes, yes, yes," she called in a monotone, and hearing a human voice snapped me out of my hallucination. Instantly the bloody vision cleared, and there was my gray boy friend Claude being raped by a gray celebrity service called Baba.

Before I could leap on her, slash her throat, and rescue Claude, their movements became convulsive, their groans united, and she collapsed against his heaving chest.

I waited, to be sure that she did not intend to cause further harm, before pulling the scarf off the lamp.

"Oh, God," Claude gasped, as if he had given up hope that help would arrive. He held her head under his chin. Baba turned her morgue shot to me and emitted a short, stifled scream. Caught red-handed in her criminal act, the rapist registered terror. Blue mascara was smudged over her depraved face, and her damp shiksa hair had died of lacquer poisoning.

"Get dressed." Claude helped his assailant to her feet. She had a boy-girl body. Legs that went straight into slim hips, a small curved behind, and surprisingly full, long-nippled tits.

"I'm sorry," she mumbled. "I'm sorry. It just happened."

"Shall I call the police?" I asked Claude. "Or should I finish her off?"

"Okay, take it easy," he said to me.

"Did she hurt you, Claude? Are you all right?"

"Don't go near her, Harriet, or I swear, I'll knock you down. Are you ready?" he asked her. They were both moving like two comedians in a speeded-up silent film. Claude was into his shirt and pants with Clark Kent dispatch, and Baba literally fell into her white regulations. They showed the wear and tear of a very busy night molesting patients in the ward.

She was shaking from satiation.

"Here," Claude said and handed her a small mountain of chains that she had previously worn around her neck and waist. So that was the weapon used on the poor rat.

She clutched the chains and stood at the door. Claude opened the door.

"Where do you think you're going?" I shouted.

"I'll take you home." He shielded her, holding her by the shoulders and guiding her out of the apartment.

I might have run after them, but I just managed to

get to safety and throw up my guts. My insides were convulsed with dry, heaving sobs, and my face was burning. I couldn't catch my breath, and my legs were turning into bananas for a change. It was all I could do to arrange for my dead body to be found decently in a bed, not draped around the bathroom fixtures.

7

I woke up feeling so bad that turning my head to read Claude's digital-clock radio remains one of my more memorable achievements. It was two thirty, and the room was saturated with the gloomy light of a rainy afternoon. I just lay on that bed, pitying Claude, because the idea of being bodily molested was too grim to wish even on him. I knew in my bones that Claude wasn't back. The reason I knew was that I was freezing, which suggested that the air conditioner had been in action all night.

I didn't have the strength to mess around with the TV set. Anyway, if they aren't burying some murdered dignitary, Saturday afternoon is the absolute bottom of the barrel. I didn't think about Claude's treachery or my suspicion that the child abuser had spent the night with Baba. When your physical system is as ravaged as mine was, everything except the necessity of breathing becomes a detail. All that concerned me was how to get to the air conditioner and turn it off before I was frozen solid. Forget it. The numbness, the drowsiness, the inability to rouse oneself, so movingly described in the diaries of Arctic cadavers, overtook me. I surrendered to the sweet embrace of eternal sleep.

When I came out of that stupor, my face was turned in the right direction, so it was without effort that I saw it had become six o'clock. The chill in the apartment was now unbearable. Leave it to the rat to arrange my destruction by the method I myself had frequently requested. Where was he?

I switched on the TV, and there before a map stood a madman doing a doctoral dissertation on the fact that it was raining. It was easy to leave him to his ranting, and I made it to the living room, fell on the air conditioner, and turned off the death machine. The lamp on the floor was a hideous reminder of the recent debacle. Where was the rodent? I appreciated his guilt, but as always, he was complicating the situation. The longer he waited to face the music, the more my divine patience ran out.

I seriously considered dressing and leaving the apartment. Let the rat crawl in shamefacedly and find me gone. That would give him something concrete to worry about. But where in that downpour, and in my weakened condition, was I going to drag myself? Better to have our scene over and done with.

What tone and position should I assume regarding his infantile behavior? I sat down on the couch and lit a Marlboro. I was still dressed in my festive fineries, adding an unbearable note of pathos to the tragedy. Tragedy? Should I treat it as a tragedy? Wasn't that giving Baba a bit more importance than the amateur home wrecker deserved? I knew, on some intuitive level, why Claude had permitted her to take advantage of him. Of course, he was proving his masculinity to me, which was nonsensical. I was more than willing to have him prove it directly. Hadn't I tried, apparently unsuccessfully, to deliver that happy piece of information? But go communicate such glad tidings to a man in the throes of sexual insecurity. On second thought, not only would I not leave the apartment, I would graciously act as though nothing had happened. I threw my untouched cigarette into a cup, fighting off the waves of nausea the smoke had provoked.

I leaned my tired, throbbing head on the back of the couch and waited. Unbelievable as it may seem, waiting for Claude had become the central activity in my life. I must have been suffering from a form of culture shock that afflicts all widely traveled Americans, as a result of which Claude had come to represent home. In the six months I'd been with him, my waiting had developed into a kind of mania. I would actually find myself waiting to hear his footsteps running up the stairs, and during his frequent catastrophe jaunts around the country, I would wait, in a reverie of waiting, for his return. Unless I am blind and deaf, he was always glad to find me waiting. I sensed that my healthy presence was a necessary balance to his obsessive interest in scab-encrusted junkies and crippled fruit pickers. He would fall into our bed like a wounded warrior, and thanks to my inexhaustible capacity for female sympathy, I would joyfully revive and nurse him. For a change, I was sitting alone, listening for footsteps, prepared to do my nursing bit.

It occurred to me that one: I should check out my face, because no one wants to be treated by a battered nurse, and two: I should probably force myself to take some nourishment. I went to the bathroom and found a mess, which I dutifully wiped up. After that degrading job, I decided to bathe and then eat. Where was he? It was becoming dark outside. All right, so he had a guilty conscience, but at least he could call?

I reconnoitered the refrigerator while the tub was filling. There were all my elaborate preparations of the previous evening, untouched by human hands. I realized I was starving and ripped a wing off one of the barbecued chickens. I put the morsel to my lips, and at that instant a most horrible flash sizzled through my brain. What if I choked on a chicken bone? A pretty sight indeed: me, blue on the kitchen floor, a chunk of chicken sticking out of my dead mouth. No, thank you. I put water in the kettle to boil. I had never heard of anyone's windpipe being blocked by a cup of coffee.

A bath, I decided, a soothing bubble bath. But some signal was interfering with the image of me soaking up relaxation in a warm tub. It was this rather unattractive vision of my bloated body found after a few undisturbed weeks of immersion. I managed, with trembling hands, to brush my teeth and wash my face. I detected a few red blotches on my skin, particularly on my eyelids. My knees weakened as I studied the unfamiliar symptoms of a wasting disease. What did I have? Why had I been so reckless as to ascribe my weakened condition to a mere hangover? What hangover? Now that I reflected on it, I had drunk very little. A few martinis and a few glasses of wine. Was that a reason to be covered with fish scales? Oh, God, what a terrible time to be alone.

Forget the lousy coffee. Who had the strength to cook? I took the carton of chocolate-chip ice cream and a spoon into my sick bed.

It was seven thirty and all was not well, unless you consider dizziness, listlessness, and ringing ears signs of well-being. I happen to know they are the signs of mononucleosis.

The only so-called entertainment on television was a monstrous hunk of boredom called The Explorers. If you could hop into your private jet and fly to Connect-icut, Channel 3 had a comedy hour. I lay in the bed, spooning ice cream into my numb mouth and periodically checking my weak pulse, compared to which a buried fakir's would register as overactive.

I suffered through these two dyke nitwits conquering the Salmon River rapids. Only God knows what their mothers had done to them. The enchanting musical duet that introduces All in the Family prevented me from hearing Claude's key turn in the lock.

"Harriet?"

For a moment, not surprisingly, I thought it was my Maker, but then recognized Claude's voice. "In here, darling."

Claude came and stood at the bedroom door. I held out my reproachless arms. "My warrior, my wonderful, brave warrior is home. You look terrible. Take off those wet things instantly, my darling, and come to bed. Your favorite show is just going on."

I ask you, could any woman have been more forgiving?

"Come into the other room," he said darkly, "I want to talk to you."

"Talk, talk, talk," I gaily chastised him. "What's there to talk about? Claude, I forgive you, I forgive you for everything." I might as well have tried my Swahili on him.

"Get out of bed."

"I don't know if I should, it seems I have mononucleosis or even leukemia," I hinted.

The brute actually reached down and yanked me out of the bed. If Claude had leukemia, believe me, he'd expect you to be all over him with juices and compresses, but a sick woman? We are expected to carry on with our duties until they do us a favor and pronounce us dead.

I followed him into the living room. He looked bad, but not bad enough. He spotted the telltale lamp on the floor, and he casually set it on the end table.

"Now," he began, "you have one day, twenty-four hours, to get out of here. I won't be staying here tonight, I have an assignment. Here's a hundred dollars." He threw a roll of bills on the coffee table. "You can check into the Chelsea Hotel, you can try the Albert, or you can drop dead. I don't care. But when I get back here tomorrow night, you'll be gone or very very sorry."

My vocal chords froze. My forgiveness speech wilted on my tongue. All the time he and Baba had been working on that announcement, I had been racking my mind for ways to forgive him.

"Claude!" I cried.

His hand shot up like a traffic cop's. "I don't want to hear one word out of you. It's taking all my self-control not to choke you."

"Choke me? I've done nothing but lie here all day worrying about you, and you'll be happy to hear that I've decided never to throw that cheap tart's name up to you. What name? Who would even believe that Baba was the name of a person?"

"Shut up," he yelled at me, and took a bottle of Scotch off a shelf and poured himself a drink. He tried it cautiously, like a swimmer sticking a toe into the icy ocean, and then swallowed the whole thing with one brave tilt of his head.

"I'm in a hurry," he said, as the drink shuddered into his belly.

"What's the rush? Where are you going? Can't we at least talk?"

"No." He left me and went to the bathroom. I ran after him. He began throwing his perfumes and deodorants into a leather kit.

I grabbed his arm to stop him. "What are you doing? Claude, don't you understand? You don't even need to apologize. I forgive you. All is forgiven."

"You didn't by any miracle get my shirts out?"

My mouth opened to emit a horrified bubble.

"I didn't think you would," he said bitterly.

It was all too much and much too fast. "I like that. That's the thanks I get for spending all of yesterday cooking and cleaning and scrubbing. What am I, your hired hand? It so happens I'm only human. I can do only so much."

"Your bondage is ending, Harriet. You no longer have to waste your remarkable intellectual gifts as my servant."

"Who's complaining? You're misinterpreting me. I love being your valet. What else would a normal woman want out of life? Okay, if you're going through a difficult period, we'll have it your way. I'll do the housekeeping, and you can work out your sexual kinks with Baba. What else are the Babas of this world created for? Have me as a confidante, a friend, a mother, if you must. But, Claude, don't end our relationship over one infidelity that as far as I'm concerned was so normal, so masculine of you, that if anything, my respect for you has increased. Hate yourself all you want, but believe me, I love you for your weaknesses."

"Housekeeping." He laughed his rotten laugh, zipping up his bag. "You've done nothing for six months but lie around the house like an irritable invalid, complaining, bitching if I ask you to open a can of soup. Six months of your devotion has driven me mad."

"But that's all over." I followed him to the living-room door. "Listen to me. There's an explanation. I didn't have it myself until this afternoon. That's what

I've been dying to tell you. It develops that I've been ill. Very ill. It's a relapse of mononucleosis. Now that we know, with proper treatment and bed rest, which is all it takes, you'll have all my energy and abilities at your beck and call. I already feel stronger from just one day in bed."

"Call the Chelsea as soon as I leave. They have lots of check-outs on Sunday."

"You're not hearing what I'm saying," I shouted into his stubborn, suicidal face. "I can't let you do this to yourself, you, with your morbid sense of duty. Don't leave me for Baba, I beg of you. She'll ruin your life."

"Let me ruin my life my way," the maniac insisted. "And Baba has nothing, absolutely nothing to do with my decision."

"Well, where the hell are you running with your perfumes? Does she have a roommate you prefer? I know how stewardesses live, in gangbangs."

He opened the door. "I'll be in Baltimore till tomorrow afternoon. They're rioting and looting there now."

"How wonderful for you."

"That's your deadline, Harriet."

The door slammed behind him, and I stood alone, stunned, hoping that for once I was having a bad dream that would end with Claude pawing me. I staggered back to the bed. Archie Bunker was doing his million-dollar takeoff on my father, which added to the unreality of Claude's explosive entrance and exit. Something informed me it had all been intolerably real. I turned down the sound and buried my hot head in the pillows. My teeth were clenched, my throat ached, and then I cried.

I cried and cried. I cried about Claude. I cried about MacDonald. I cried about Paris. I cried about the American Hospital. I cried about the goons who had forced me on the plane and had sent me back to this concentration camp. I cried until I became afraid that I would never stop finding things to cry about, and then it stopped.

I didn't feel refreshed by what's generally called a good cry. On the contrary, I felt increasingly hopeless. In spite of my waves of despair, I stayed up writing lists and making plans, until there was daylight in the window.

If I told you what I went through the next day to change a stinking lock, you'd think I was talking about the lock that locks Fort Knox, not the lock in a run-down tenement.

I woke up later than scheduled, because I was so afraid of oversleeping, I couldn't fall asleep. All I have to do is imagine something and it happens. I lit a cigarette and turned on the TV, collecting the lists strewn all over the bed. There, on the tube, was a panel of blacks, demanding back payment for three hundred years of tap dancing. Lots of luck. Then I knew with a horrified seizure of total recall that today was Sunday. Even though I had suffered through a ghastly Saturday, I had overlooked the coming of Sunday. All of my carefully laid plans, my shopping list made with visions of the A&P at my disposal, were shot. I felt my clarity mounting into hysteria. Could I find a locksmith on Sunday? I sprinted out of the bed and dived into the Yellow Pages.

I almost wept with relief when I saw that they were available for night time and Sunday emergencies. I carried the telephone to the couch, lit a cigarette, and started dialing numbers. There wasn't even a heart-warming answering service to appeal to. It was all re-cordings and beeps and listening units and machines waiting to record my name and number. There were no more people out there, just machines.

I ripped off my tie-dyed skirt and Mexican blouse, filled the tub, and plunged in. The water was chilling but reviving. I realized the place was hot again. The rain hadn't broken the heat wave.

I was out of the tub when the first machine called back. I had my story ready. To wit: I was this extraor-dinarily proper married woman who had been mugged and purse-snatched by a gang of rapists the previous evening. My devoted husband, currently in Baltimore, had insisted that I put in a new lock with all possible speed.

"I have one emergency before you," the indifferent male on the other end informed me. "I can be at your place in one hour."

"One hour," I shrieked.

"It's the best I can do. Don't worry, lady, street mug-gers aren't house thieves. They're two different breeds."

"But my mugger may know a house thief," I per-sisted.

"If you're so frightened, wait in a neighbor's apartment for an hour."

"All right, an hour, but please, no later, it's urgent."

What I didn't know was that he intended to keep me on the phone for an hour. What kind of lock did I want? Did I have a wooden or a metal door? Did I need a police lock or a pick-resistant cylinder?

I felt nervous tears filling my eyes. "Please, I don't have a Ph.D. in locks. Bring me a lock that will lock with a key and keep the muggers out."

He still hadn't tortured me sufficiently. He launched into the economics of the affair. It was twenty dollars for emergency service, plus the price of new equipment. I had to expect it to cost fifty dollars.

"I have the money, just get here." Fifty dollars for a piece of tin and half an hour's work? Small wonder the intellectual community in America was shrinking.

It was already one thirty when I got into a pair of relatively fresh white jeans and a blue-and-white-striped T-shirt. I peeled fifty dollars off the roll Claude had thrown on the coffee table and ran, with the rest of the money clutched in my hand, to the delicatessen on Bleecker Street.

Halfway there, I discovered I'd forgotten my shopping list. There wasn't time to go back for it. Karl Marx himself had never prayed harder for a miserable riot to develop into a revolution.

The streets were disgusting; the heat, cooking stew in the curbs again, and the usual lynch mob looking for a cause. Then the delicatessen! Every hoarder in New York was jammed into the place, as if starting tomorrow an embargo were going to descend on the city. My siege, as I figured it, would last two weeks, by which time Claude would be thoroughly disenchanted with Baba.

I grabbed a wire basket and started filling it with necessities. Two large jars of Nescafé. Two large jars of Cremora. Four vitamin C-packed quarts of orange juice. Two loaves of Levy's rye bread. One pound of butter. Two dozen eggs. Fourteen cans of tuna fish and, to keep my spirits from sagging, a half-dozen flat tins of imported antipasto packed in virgin olive oil, which were conveniently displayed beside the tuna fish or I might never have thought of them. That basket was filled. I scooped up another. Dinner time. Seven frozen TV turkey dinners, seven frozen deep-fried shrimp dinners, a jar of tartar sauce, a large Hellmann's mayonnaise, four packages of Hydrox cookies, and just in case the blockade extended beyond my calculations, I asked the counterman for one pound of freshly prepared lobster salad and a half pound of Nova Scotia, which required six bagels and a quick dash to the other side of the store for a large cream cheese. Then I waited on a line that crept along, silently and passively, as though the bums were getting fed free. Tears of exasperation stung my eyes. It was finally my turn.

The sage at the cash register had something to say. "Are you entertaining an orphan asylum?"

"Hurry," I urged him, fighting back tears.

He rang and he rang and he rang up some more. The bill came to $52.28.

"I don't have enough money." Sobs broke loose from my tight chest.

"Easy, darling," the capitalist consoled me. "It's not the end of the world. How much money do you have?"

"Fifty dollars." I held a fistful of money up to him.

The lynch mob behind me was growing restless. Was I perhaps their chosen victim?

"So I'll take off two dollars' worth of groceries. You can live with only four antipasto, no?"

I could have kissed his hands for that unexpected display of wisdom.

"What don't you want?"

"It doesn't matter. Take back anything." My tears dried up. After all, maybe ten days with Baba would be sufficient?

He did the recount, and this time I won the election. My order filled two cardboard cartons.

"What time should we deliver?" my friend inquired, relieving me of my fifty dollars.

"As soon as possible. You see," I said, enjoying a flash of inspiration, "it's for my wedding party, and I'm going to be married in an hour."

"Mazeltov," he congratulated me in an unfamiliar tongue.

I raced back to the apartment and up the stairs, for once disregarding Rhoda-Regina's complexes.

I got to my door and screamed when I realized I didn't have the keys. I hadn't even bothered with my Cretan shoulder bag, which generally accompanied me everywhere. I reconstructed the terrible moment when I'd grabbed the money in my hand and locked myself out of the apartment. I could hear the phone ringing; that had to be all the emergency locksmiths in America. I sat down on the top step, put my head in my hands, and my lamentations filled the hall.

I didn't keep track of how long I cried, but it wasn't brief. Finally, there was the slow, casual echo of this sadist with a black metal box, slowly mounting the stairs. I wiped my face.

He got to my landing and read off a slip of paper he was holding. "Are you the Mary who called for a locksmith?"

"No. I'm her heir. She was buried this afternoon."

"You could have waited for me in the apartment."

"I'm locked out," I shrieked.

He laboriously reread his idiot sheet.

"It doesn't say anything about a lockout? We're going to have to break in?"

"So what? So we'll break in. We're getting rid of the old lock anyway."

His young blond blue-eyed mean face tightened into a frown. I had heard rumors about Ilse Koch giving birth to a son in prison, but I'd never hoped to meet the boy.

"Do you have any proof that this is your apartment?"

My voice rose hysterically. "I called you. My name is Mary. I'm sitting here locked out. You think I'm some sort of lunatic who just goes around changing other people's locks?"

"I have to have proof. Do you have a driver's license, a bill, something to identify you?"

"My purse was snatched."

"Is there a neighbor who can identify you?"

I thought fleetingly of this vengeful deity who pursued me and was now supplying Rhoda-Regina with an airtight opportunity for revenge. No, Officer, I never saw her before in my life.

"I'm a married woman and I live here with my husband." I sobbed, the tears in my head overflowing for a change.

I heard footsteps coming up the stairs. I closed my eyes and prepared to faint.

When I opened them, there was this Puerto Rican delivery boy, balancing my cartons of groceries, doing a full Egyptian slave up the steep pyramid.

"He knows me," I shouted.

"You know this woman?" Ilse's boy demanded. How proud she would have been, could she have lived to enjoy his cruelty.

"Sure," my Puerto Rican savior said.

"Does she live in this apartment?"

"Sure."

"Is that delivery for her?"

"Sure."

God bless him for his mastery of the English language.

"Okay," the Nazi decided, "I'll change the lock."

It took him almost an hour of drilling, hammering, and cursing to get the old lock off, and then almost as long to replace it. He tried the new one a few times with a beautiful, shiny, new key.

"You're set," he finally said.

"Thank you, thank you, thank you."

He helped me carry the cartons into the apartment. "That'll be sixty-five dollars."

"I can't pay you," I screamed. "I only have fifty. You told me fifty."

"But, lady, that didn't include breaking in."

Crying was beginning to be my middle name.

"I'll bring you the other fifteen. I swear on my mother's grave, you'll have the rest of the money by tomorrow. But please, I beg of you, leave now. I'm very upset from my mugging. Please, have mercy on me."

He shrugged. "Give me the fifty."

I scooped up the money on the coffee table and pressed it into his dirty hands.

"Tomorrow, Mary, no later. We've got your name, number, and address. No money and I'll have to remove the lock. It's company policy."

"You'll have it, you'll have it. Do I look like a criminal?"

I locked him out with my new lock and fell on the couch, gasping for breath. I lit a cigarette and, with that automatic act, realized that I had neglected to buy two cartons of cigarettes, the number-one item on my shopping list. I burst into frustrated, enraged, indignant tears.

I couldn't move from the couch. Not to unload the groceries. Not to lie down. Not to turn on the air conditioner. I was nailed, crucified to the couch. I ignored the ringing telephone.

Claude's footsteps, when I heard them, were meaningless to me. I listened to his useless key tampering with my new lock.

"Harriet? Harriet, are you in there?"

The slow-witted adulterer continued to struggle with my new lock.

I heard his fists banging on the door.

"Let me in. Open this door, you miserable cunt."

I sat riveted on the couch, terrified that his adrenaline would give him the strength to break down the door and murder me.

The pounding, this time his shoulder trying to crash through, resumed, and finally, bruised and beaten, he gave up. I listened to his retreating footsteps, and still I sat there, immobilized.

The bottle of Scotch was staring at me, till I got the message and filled Claude's empty glass. The whiskey helped. After a few minutes I could move, but not from the couch. The telephone was ringing again, and this time I knew it was Claude.

You can imagine how thrilled I was to hear Maxine's war whoop.

"Harriet," she shrieked, ecstatic with self-importance, "Claude called me and told me about you locking him out. Is it true, Harriet? Have you gone completely mad?"

I didn't answer.

"Harriet, you can't do that. It's against the law. Jerry spoke to Claude, and he told him. Claude has the right to stop any cop on the street, bring him up, and force you off his property."

It was typical of Maxine to credit Jerry with her own vicious betrayals.

I found my voice. "Fink. Filthy fink, dirty Jew, turning on your own kind."

"But it's illegal, Harriet. You're trespassing. Claude said he gave you money to go to a hotel. What do you want from the poor guy, his blood?"

The phone became welded to my hand. "You and your fat ugly husband should only hang from a tree in Israel, Judas, murderer." I slammed the receiver down. I clutched my head, wailing and moaning at the conspiracy of hate that surrounded me. Soon I heard them, the entire Gestapo, marching up the steps. I spilled half the Scotch on the table, clumsily trying to refill my glass.

"Are you sure she's in there?" a gruff voice asked.

"She's in there."

"Open up, this is the law." They must teach them, in those SS academies, how to pound on a door and freeze the will, the hope, the life of the trapped victim.

"Open up, or I'll break the door in."

How often had my people heard those savage words? Often enough for me to rise like a doomed automaton, walk to the door, and unlock the new lock.

Three gorillas pushed their way into the room. I counted Claude, Charles, and an unfamiliar thug in dark blue.

"Miss," the thug said, his light-blue eyes slits of graft and corruption, "you are trespassing on this legal tenant's property. If you do not leave peaceably, this gentleman is entitled to a court order requiring your appearance before a judge."

"Gentleman? Where? Who? That one," I pointed at Claude, "is a sexual pervert, and that one," I accused Charles, "is a drug addict."

"Miss, don't make trouble. I am not empowered to forcibly evict you, but I suggest that you leave quietly. Changing the lock represents violation of private property."

"Officer," Claude said to the generously bribed henchman, "I'd like to go in and pack her things."

"Don't you dare destroy my belongings." I followed him into the bedroom.

Claude threw my goatskin sack on the bed and started shoving the contents of the bentwood into its flabby belly. He worked quickly, not talking.

"Claude, wait, what are you doing? Has Charles drugged you? The fiend, the jealous faggot."

Claude spoke. "Charles has his car here. I won't just throw you out, in your condition. We'll drive you to the Chelsea."

"I have no money."

"What happened to the hundred dollars?" Charles, hearing Claude's thundering abuse, came to the bedroom door.

"How should I know? I had a hamburger at Joe's. I bought a pack of cigarettes. It's gone."

"I'm not giving you another cent."

Charles addressed his lover in French. "What's the problem?"

"She's blackmailing me for more money."

Charles dug a wad of money out of his pocket. "This is no time to worry about money. I'll give her money. The important thing is to get her out."

It was a small miracle to discover that there was a way to say money isn't important in the French language.

"No," I protested in English. "I don't want your blood money. The nickels and dimes you've cadged out of addicted schoolchildren."

The cop crowded into the bedroom. "What's the problem?"

"Listen to their funny accents. What are they saying? They're two foreign spies. Do they have the legal right to throw an American citizen into the gutter?"

"Are those all her things?" the hood politely asked his boss.

"No. I absolutely refuse to leave without my tuna fish. And I'll take the electric can opener," I said defiantly.

Claude had the audacity to roll his eyes at Charles, and then he forced the roll of bills into my jeans pocket.

"Don't lose it," he said with his revolting French caution. And then: "Ready?"

"One more tiny detail, Claude. Just for the record, I want you to know you're not throwing me out. In the last six months I've done everything humanly possible to save you. I give up. I want it absolutely clear, I've tried, but now I'm leaving you."

8

I DON'T know how long I slept, because when I awoke in my solitary cell, of the many things I did not see, most conspicuously absent was a digital-clock radio. Go tell the time, in a sunless room, from shadows on the wall. For all I knew, I was Rudolf Hess rising and shining in Spandau, because if he's as crazy and subject to persecution manias as his attorneys purport, what worse thing could he wish on himself than to wake up as me? I lay in my narrow, lumpy bed, calmly aware that the thin, tufted mattress had crippled me for life. A dancer could have an airtight damage suit, but a non-professional such as myself, who simply preferred a healthy spinal column for personal reasons, had no case. I couldn't find the energy to turn my head. Had anyone, I wondered, ever been this tired? There was a recent collection of pictures in my head, vivid and meaningless. Claude throwing my bags into the rear of Charles's car. A hotel lobby ugly with paintings, hanging metal objects, and fluorescent light fixtures. A skinny, balding night clerk ignoring me and handing Claude a key. Claude unlocking a door and dumping my worldly goods on a green, blue, and yellow linoleum floor worn brown in spots.

All through the room, cracks and burns exposed an underlayer of barren brown that was spreading as though blight had struck the skimpy surfaces. A yellowish lampshade next to the bed had succumbed to a half century of forty-watt bulbs and displayed its diseased patches of brown. There was no question in my mind that whatever had afflicted the room was contagious and would get to me next.

There was something going on in my stomach that could have been hunger, except its path swerved off when it reached my chest and I knew it wasn't hunger. My dry mouth and closed throat guaranteed my feeling had nothing to do with food. It was about being alone at a new front, and my cowardly stomach was trying to desert to a neutral corner. It could pull and crawl and slip around all it wanted, but it wasn't going any place without the rest of me.

Questions and arguments began to form in my head and dwindled off after a few timid words. There are times when I'd rather converse with a crazed mugger than reason with myself. Anyway, what good are questions when you can't use the answers? One of the most unfair things in life is how quickly the present slinks into the past and, once there, becomes part of ancient history. Yesterday was gone, as surely as if it had been mine or Cleopatra's. What difference did it make to anyone, with the possible exception of M-G-M, if I was thrown into this cell, because I'd lost Egypt or lost Claude? No one had ever been more alone than I. Prisoners were waking up with other prisoners, attentive guards rattling their bars, their days blissfully arranged. Cancer patients were waking up in cancer wards, surrounded by the intimate groans of the dying, nurses and doctors busy helping them to die clean. Blacks in their ghettos were waking up in crowded beds, pushing arms and feet out of each other's faces, fighting for space. Only I was left out, alone, suspended between sleep and emptiness with nothing to fight and nowhere to be. Had anyone ever been more irrelevant, more excluded from the human celebration?

I sat at the edge of the bed with my feet planted in a dusty green rose. I touched a tuna-fish can with my toes. Hi. I took inventory. In one corner of the room was a sink, chipped and freckled brown. Above it was a square, framed mirror, the glass as polluted as the Hudson River. I expected to see a poisoned fish float across its seltzer surface. A dark green, half-raised window shade was reflected in the bubbles. Next to the sink was a waist-high, ptomaine-infested refrigerator, the door hanging on rusted hinges. On the wall facing the bed was a long, narrow, recklessly carved table, circa Bronx Bavarian. At either end of the table, pushed against the wall, was a straight-backed wooden kitchen chair with a yellow-plastic seat. It occurred to me that the room was excessively suicide-proof. No bathtub to slash your wrists in. No beams to hang from. The windows were painted shut to discourage impulsive leaps. A gun could do the job, but that was a man's way.

I went to the mirror and discovered that my face was melting. A towel would have been a luxury, as would a bar of soap, a toothbrush, toothpaste, not to speak of a place to pee other than the crummy basin. Unlike the Empress of Iran, I am not generally accompanied by a portable water closet. With trembling fingertips I arranged my natural gypsy shag to cover as much of my face as it could.

Would you believe it, after forcing myself to dress, I was afraid to open the door and leave the room? I sat on the wooden chair, my hands clenched in front of me, my heart pounding, as if the hall, the stairway, the lobby were steps to the gallows. If only I could think. But how could I think with the inside of my head boiling like a pot of spaghetti?

To appease the monsters below, I confined the tuna-fish cans, the Nescafé, the Cremora, and the mayonnaise to the rotting refrigerator. I searched for an outlet. A person with an electric can opener can't be all bad. I'd buy a few pictures, simple rustic scenes, scrub the drapes, sweep up the butts, invest in a cheerful bedspread, paint the chairs hospital white, strip and wax the table, maybe a little round hand-braided rug at the foot of the bed, lots of fragrant, fresh flowers. Mystery Girl Transforms Broomcloset into Cozy Retreat.

A plan was forming. First the pharmacy, buy lots of soap and brushes, orange sticks, toothpaste, pomades, bubble bath, night creams, be a debutante radiant with cleanliness. Who is she? I don't know, but she's the cleanest person I've ever seen.

I walked to the door, and my guiding angel reminded me to put on my sandals. The corridors with their marble floors and vaulting ceilings were designed to accommodate a state funeral. My steps echoed along the empty tomb, the solitary sound bouncing off the filthy walls. I held my head high as I descended the Napoleonic staircase. The reason for my regal posture, I noticed with a shudder, was a stiffness, a rigidity in fact, from the base of my skull to the back of my heels. Is this, I wondered, the onslaught of spinal meningitis? Is an iron lung, a mirror tilted to reflect the world, my destiny? Who wouldn't feel a tremor of fear at such a horrible prospect? I felt my legs buckling under me and got to the front desk just in time to grab at it and prevent myself from crumbling into an unconscious mass.

"I am the occupant of 228," I volunteered. "I guess I ought to register."

The desk clerk didn't answer but started running his finger down a large ledger. "Are you Harriet . . ." he began, but I stopped him. Even under stress, they won't find me napping.

"No. She merely made the reservation for me." We both smiled at the silly game we were forced to play. "My name is Stephanie; however," I signed the register, "if you should happen to get a call or a letter for my friend Harriet, I am the only person in America who knows how to reach her." He ran his coroner's finger, gray and bloodless, along the page.

"Your room is paid up until the twenty-second of September." To complete the comedy, he added, "Is everything satisfactory?"

"It depends," I said haughtily, "on what you're satisfying."

Well, the first hurdle was met. I think there is nothing more reviving for the human spirit than to attack a problem head-on. My spine derigidified. The lobby, like the halls, was immense. If not for the language, I would have sworn I was in the Winter Palace at St. Petersburg. Keeping my eyes fixed on the revolving door a good quarter of a mile away, I captured in my peripheral vision a collection of long-haired freaks, all fringed and beaded, slumped on red benches, gently caressing guitar cases and amplifiers. I sensed how mortifying it would be to collapse in a mindless heap in the middle of that funk and quickened the tempo. I sailed through the revolving door.

I escaped down Seventh Avenue. It was very pleasant and friendly if you happened to be a native of San Juan. Being I am who I am, I couldn't read one sign or recognize one fruit or vegetable in the grocery windows. Most disturbing, I couldn't understand the numerous proposals and tongue cluckings flung at me. Don't get too far from the hotel, a concerned inner voice guided me. Returning to Twenty-third Street was a bit like getting off the boat. My survival instincts led me to a Horn & Hardart, where there was no nice lady dispensing handfuls of nickels, because, due to a prohibitive investment in plastic flowers and genuine-brick wallpaper, the nickel as legal tender had become as obsolete as beads and stones. The tables were filled with a lot of people drowning their sorrows in glasses of water.

For some reason, as I pushed my tray along the counter of steaming foods, I found myself reminiscing about the meals I had choked down at my mother's table. My mother, the High Priestess of Duggan's cupcakes, was famous for never being hungry. She never sat down for a meal, yet weighed in at a mighty two hundred pounds. "I don't know," she would say, jabbing a fork into the gray pile of chopped liver on my plate, "I just have no appetite. Is it good?" she'd ask me, as if I lived in her mouth. Good? It was chopped liver, and chopped liver could taste only one way. Her way. My father, across from me, would look up at his wife and in code request a Pepsi-Cola. He was to Pepsi-Cola what she was to Duggan's cupcakes. She would sigh her way to the icebox and back, watch him empty the bottle, and then race him for the glass. She always won, because not being a juggler, he lost a split second putting the bottle down and reaching for the fix with his right hand.

"Terrible," she'd say, guzzling his drink down. "I don't know how you can take this poison." How we escaped acute malnutrition with this woman doing all our eating for us is a problem I leave to medical science.

"Ma," I'd say, "sit down and eat."

"Me eat?" She'd snatch the roll out of my hand and

rip it open with her teeth. "Are you crazy? When do I ever eat? If I ate the way you and your father eat, I'd explode."

"Ethel," said my enchanting dinner companion, "is there more Pepsi-Cola?"

"Six bottles you've drunk today." She'd give him the countdown, washing my bread down with the few dregs left in the bottom of his glass. "Who can keep up with you? Look," she'd point dramatically into the kitchen, "I order the poison by the case." And sure enough, stacked in the kitchen was a monument, a pyramid of empty cases.

When my mother was not eating, she kept herself occupied by not sleeping. Each morning, upon opening my eyes, I would discover her face hanging over me, haggard from sixteen hours of not sleeping. "What do you want for dinner tonight?" she'd demand, her voice thick with tension. While the rest of the gluttonous world mindlessly slept, Ethel lay staring into the darkness, pondering what to cook. Needless to say, I'd get whatever slop the institution was serving that day. When she slapped those burned little meatballs in front of me, I knew it was Tuesday, the way Columbus knew those grinning extras were Indians.

I studied the vats of stewing garbage offered by the cafeteria. An emaciated alcoholic, who looked as though the rising steam had dissolved his flesh, waited for me to make a decision.

"You're holding up the line, miss." His old voice came drifting out of the vapors, and sure enough, behind me was a snarling mob of tray carriers ready to break into a prison riot. Being normal, it's not easy for me to make free choices under that kind of pressure. Rather than be lacerated by the forks the inmates had cleverly sharpened into daggers, I panicked and pointed to a pot of bubbling glue, which turned out to be the most inedible of all comestibles, tongue, its taste-buds stiff with rigor mortis. He handed me the plate, and I placed it in the center of my tray and led the parade toward the desserts. I selected a wedge of mincemeat pie, in order to establish my patriotism. She is an American, my tray arrogantly declared, and I flashed a five-dollar bill at the cashier. She smiled at me. I found an empty table near the window.

Not having been trained in cafeteria etiquette, I had neglected to equip myself with eating utensils. When I returned with two forks and a glass of polluted water, I found an intruder seated at my table. In front of him were the following foods: a brownie, chocolate pudding, a scoop of chocolate ice cream, a chocolate eclair, and a slice of devil's-food cake. I pushed the tongue away from me and concentrated on the mysteries of the mincemeat pie.

"Can't eat it?" the boy said, gesturing toward my coagulated plate of tongue. I wondered just how I should respond to his seemingly innocuous statement. If I ignored him, he might attack me on the spot. If I answered him, I was on my way to rape and mutilation. The sensible ruse was to charm him out of his ferocious intentions.

"Tongue makes me nauseous," I frankly replied.

"How come you ordered it?"

"Oh, well." I laughed. "I forgot about my aversion."

"I'm hip," he said. "You gotta keep the line moving."

"The fact is," I informed him, "I happen to be an automat inspector."

"Automat inspector?" He clearly had never met one of us before and was impressed.

"What do you inspect?" he asked politely, clearing his chocolate-lined throat.

"Well, you know, it depends on the complaints we receive. I'm in food." I gave him a clue.

"Like if the cooking isn't up to standard?"

"Oh, we don't care about standards. At least," I corrected myself, "not in regards to the cooking."

"Like if the food is bad?"

"You're getting warm. Listen, I'll tell you something very few people outside the organization know. Statistically, in one month we are responsible for more ptomaine poisoning than all the canned-soup companies rack up in a year."

"Wow," he said.

"If all those poisoned people got together, which of course they can't, but if their heirs joined forces, I guess," I threw up my hands, "well, I guess they could just about pick anyone they wanted for President."

"Ahhh, you're putting me on," he said.

"Listen, we try to avoid it," I loyally defended the company. "That's my job. I mean, for instance, suppose we get a report that an egg-salad sandwich has been sitting in its glass cage for a year and a half. Now, we don't want anyone to eat that sandwich; at the same time, it's a hell of a lot of glass boxes to keep track of."

"Desserts must be safe." He mournfully regarded his untouched eclair.

"Ha. If we could drop our desserts on Vietnam, I swear we'd end the war, if, that is, anyone was left to sign the country over to us. Look at my mincemeat pie," I advised him. "You see those green specks on it?"

"I don't see green specks." He stood up abruptly. "I'm late," he mumbled. He seemed to have misplaced my eyes, and his glance skimmed the top of my head. I had naturally grown quite attached to him. After all, in a manner of speaking, he was the only acquaintance I had in New York.

"Why don't you have a cup of coffee? I'll treat. We get it on the house, you know. I promise, we've never had a coffee fatality."

"I don't drink coffee, but thanks anyway. Well, happy inspecting."

"What's your name?" I called after him, but he vanished out of the picture as if someone had switched channels. It was my first taste of what people mean when they talk about New York being a cold city. Brrr. Why, if I met a food inspector anywhere, in Athens, in Paris, in Prague, I'd listen to him forever.

A bum in Dr. Kildare's blood-smeared ducks shuffled over and mechanically wiped the table with a cloth that looked as if it had been dipped in extract of smallpox infection.

Out on the street, I searched for the boy. Only then did I realize how intense the attraction had been. Had he expected me to follow him? If only I could find him and tell him that I didn't understand the mating customs of his generation. Why hadn't I at least told him where I was staying? These reflections led me back to the door of the hotel, and I entered.

There was a new clerk on duty, this one in complete drag, so I acted dumb and said, "Miss, are there any messages for my friend Harriet?"

"What room?"

"Two twenty-eight."

She checked an empty box. "Nothing."

"Did anyone call and not leave a name?"

"Not since I've been on duty."

"Well," I directed her, "in case anyone calls and doesn't leave a name, please don't take the message."

The elevator filled with people, but not my adorable lost boy. Nor was he leaning on the wall outside my room. Unlocking my door, I prepared myself not to find him in my bed. As usual, my expectation was confirmed. I lay down on the empty bed and remembered all the things I'd forgotten to buy: toothpaste, soap, toothbrush. It was becoming dark in my room. I closed my eyes. It was probably wise of me to have released the boy before he became hopelessly involved. Wouldn't his youth, initially appealing, ultimately bore me? Was I prepared to educate him to my level?

I lifted myself wearily from the bed and approached the refrigerator. You could get lead poisoning looking at it. I opened a can of tuna fish. By now it was dark. I was missing Flip Wilson. So what. Let the world watch Flip Wilson while I, an exceptional person by almost any standards, died a slow, agonizing death from mercury poisoning. I left the empty tuna-fish can on top of the refrigerator. I lay down. Tomorrow I'd return to the automat, give the boy another chance, rip off a few forks, a spoon, a knife, conduct a meaningful life.

9

I woke up fast and scared. My chest felt as though King Kong were curled up on it, taking a nap. It was hot and still in the room. I heard a strange sound and discovered it was me, panting, as if I'd come running out of my sleep carrying this great weight. I was afraid to open my eyes and afraid not to, which somewhat limited my options. I thought if I opened my eyes I would see something horrible, but if I didn't, the unseen presence, filling me with a hysterical apprehension, would get me anyway. When I discovered I couldn't open my eyes or, for that matter, my mouth, my decision was made, and I struggled to see, to call out, to move, to lift the lid entrapping me in darkness and silence. Was I asleep, half asleep, or dying? If I could just manage one movement or one word, I would be totally awake and saved. A twitch, a blink, would be enough, but even that small gesture took an impossibly gigantic effort. My body had hardened into a stone effigy. My mind, lucid and frantic, demanded that I relax into the paralysis, that to fight it was to die. My only hope was to surrender and float to the top of the darkness. Easier said than done. I lay there defeated and miraculously the evil spell lifted and my eyelids worked. Lucky me, to go through that hell in order to find myself in the dank, soul-eroding atmosphere of the Chelsea. Something was terribly wrong. At first I didn't allow myself to recognize the symptoms, but how long can you fight reality? The irony. I was having what my own mother had anticipated throughout her married life, to wit, a fatal heart attack.

My left arm, from my fingertips to my soaking-wet arm socket, was throbbing with the most excruciating shocks of pain. To imagine moving my arm was an act of indescribable heroism. My entire body, still clothed in its classic jeans-and-shirt outfit, was so drenched that I could have been treading blood in a pool of the same. An invisible serpent circled and crushed my heaving chest in a deadly cold wet grip. I could have kidded myself and pretended I wasn't having a heart attack, that my arm had simply remained asleep, as though it were my habit to wake up in pieces. I preferred to face the gravity of my condition. I don't have to tell you what a picnic interns have with unclaimed bodies. I chose to fight, to secure medical attention while still technically alive.

I refrained from useless cries for help. Why supply the sexual perverts in the adjoining room with a cheap thrill? I rose from the bed and hauled myself through the humid darkness that rushed about me like a swollen river. I dragged myself to the door, cradling my stricken arm in my good arm, which made opening the door an Olympic feat for which I expect no gold medals. God knows how I managed to do it, but I found myself dizzy and nauseous in the wide, ugly boulevard of a hall. The halls were unnaturally silent and empty, dimly lit, the air foul but less stifling than in my narrow cell. The walls were lined with tightly locked doors. I had the queasy feeling that I was the sole survivor of a radiation disaster, soon to join my fellow victims, or worse yet, that I had already succumbed and death was nothing more than a clever imitation of life, starring a cast of one. As these frivolous speculations were bombarding my aching head, one of the mute doors opened just wide enough to allow a thin figure to slip into the hall. I couldn't determine its sex, but coronary cases can't be fussy. The essential thing was to find help, not romance. Still, it's nice to know if you're appealing to a potential rapist-mugger or a void of female vanity.

The being before me was superthin and bleached as a Kleenex. Long black hanks of lifeless hair floated around a skeletal face. I was reminded of a Japanese horror movie that Claude had dragged me to, where the hero, a samurai of sorts, persistently makes love to an enchanting Oriental vision, who invariably transforms into a bag of bones topped by a hank of dead black hair, which drove me and the samurai out of our minds. Naturally Claude found it all beautiful and significant. You couldn't torture enough Japs for his refined tastes.

I called to the apparition, "Hey, hey, you."

Two large, illuminated eye sockets turned blindly in my direction.

"Come over here a minute, please." If a cadaver can be said to have a facial expression, then you'd have to call this one frightened. My voice apparently intruded on whatever reveries visit ghosts in long, empty corridors. The specter sniffed nervously, its gossamer hair falling fine as a crepe veil over its emaciated face.

"Please," I repeated, not too sure what I'd say if it decided to approach me. All I knew was that male, female, human, or spirit, I had to make contact. By then I had established it was masculine, if you can use that designation for someone whose ten fingers are jingling a delicate tune made by countless tiny bell rings vibrating against each other. Even from where I stood, I could smell him; a heavy, heady, penetrating odor of incense and musk exuded from his unique garments. He was the most aromatic and decorated person I'd ever seen. Every square inch of his blue jeans was painted or embroidered or written on. He was so covered with buttons and messages, I guess he could have been sunk in a time capsule for future generations to interpret like the Dead Sea Scrolls.

"You talking to me?" His tinkling hand supplied the musical accompaniment. The expression of total alarm never left his face.

"Listen," I said, "I'm not going to hurt you. As a matter of fact, it's just the opposite. I need your help."

"Victor sent you," he said tonelessly, staying a good ten paces away from me. "Well?" he demanded, putting his musical hands on his narrow hips and doing some kind of imitation of an angry person. "What bullshit threats has he dreamed up now?" Then he seemed to become terrified at his aggression. "He can't get me back," he said, his voice going sour. "Tell him my parents know everything and they're ready to go to the police if he or any of his lousy slaves hassle me. I just told that to Roger and he promised me," his defense got thick with tears, "he gave me his word, his rotten fink word, that Victor loved me and was praying for the day when I would regain my health and voluntarily return to his table. His table," he coughed out in a crazy brief laugh. "I like that."

I attempted to end his monologue.

"Is that your room?" I cordially inquired. "Because, if so, we're neighbors. That's my room." I thumbed the door behind me. "But it was so boiling hot in there, I made a narrow escape out here. Is your room as small and crummy as mine? Are all the rooms in this dump cubbyholes? You know, you won't believe it, but I actually imagined I was having a heart attack. Luckily, it turned out to be just an attack of suffocation. Do you by any chance have an air conditioner in your room? You look very cool."

"You know it's not my room," he said, stamping his sandaled foot and giving me another dose of his weird brand of mock anger. It was as though he had no expressions, aside from terror, but had practiced the others and could perform all the appropriate gestures.

"What's your angle, Miss Innocence? I may be crazy,"

he said triumphantly, with a proud sweep of his dandelion hair. "All the specialists in New York agree on that, but I'm not stupid."

"I'm very sorry. I didn't mean to insult your intelligence, but I really don't know what you're talking about. For instance, I never even heard of Victor or Roger before."

"Oh, sure." His skull grin stretched, doing strange things to his sharp nose. "It's all coincidence. I come out from seeing Roger and just happen to find you cooling off in the hall at one o'clock."

"One o'clock," I repeated with horror. "You mean it's only one o'clock?" I had hoped that at least it was the afternoon of the next day. At this rate, if each night of my life took an endless year to pass, my aging process was going to accelerate disastrously.

He backed off from me. "Go ahead," he dared me. "Go report to Roger. Tell him I could not be bullied. Tell him Victor can send an army of harpies after me, the furies, but he won't get me back." With that he raced down the hall, smelling and sounding like an agitated harem.

It didn't occur to me to follow, because one: I doubted my capacity to break through his obsessions, and two: the door, the same door, had opened, releasing another exotic creature. This time I heard the unmistakable sounds of an intimate party: low voices, soft bongos, subdued laughter. I almost had to refer to a previous life to remember the last soiree I'd attended, Claude's idea of a pleasant evening being to sit around with a gang of refugees, rhapsodizing over their last home-cooked meal. In Paris, you don't know if it's a party till you see who's stuck with the check.

From the evidence of the departing guests, I concluded that I was missing a fancy-dress ball. This one was so ludicrously female that I could have sworn she was a man. A frail man who had endured one face full of sand too many and had opted to go the other way, the Veronica Lake way.

A sheet of platinum hair covered one half of her face, which was just as well, because if the hidden eye required the workmanship of the public eye, then please, lay me on my back and let me paint the Sistine Chapel.

Getting up close to her, I saw that she had decorated her eye with thousands of electric-blue tentacles, thereby turning one half of her face into an octopus. Still I retained my customary optimism and spoke as though to a normal person. I have found that some of the worst nut cases are so appreciative of my tolerance that they snap into momentary sanity.

"Excuse me," I said politely, "but would you happen to know if someone named Roger is giving a party in that room you just came out of?" Her octopus eye gleamed at me. She struggled to separate her heavily coated lips.

"Party?" she said, making a small popping sound, due to air rushing into her vacuum. "Roger doesn't give parties."

"But a friend of mine, whom I happened to meet recently, invited me to a party, and I know he said it was in Roger's room."

Veronica's face underwent elaborate spasms, which caused me to believe that she was having a stroke, but it developed into a yawn, dangerously constricted by her self-seal mouth. Mortified by her social lapse, she stiffened her features into their previous immobility and marched away without so much as a goodbye. At least our limited exchange had moved me to the opposite side of the hall, and there I was, sick and friendless, before Roger's door.

Since I am cursed with this British reserve when it comes to intruding on anyone's privacy, I stood outside that door I don't know how long, trying to choose between emergency and discretion. All of my symptoms had returned with such renewed vigor, you'd think they'd been out for a refreshing drink. I was sweating, nauseous, trembling, and my poor hyperventilating heart pounding in my chest involuntarily became my fist pounding on the door. The bongos stopped. I was amazed to hear myself sob, "Please, please let me in."

By that time the door was opened, slowly, as if furniture were piled up against it, by a tall girl wearing Susan Hayward's red wig and negligee. I noticed a tiny silver spoon hanging from her neck on a thin leather cord.

"It's not Libby," she said over her shoulder.

"Who is it?" I heard a man ask.

"Some chick freaking out." She moved to slam the door in my face.

"Please," I stopped her. "I must see Roger."

"What do you want with Roger?"

"I'm sick. Call an ambulance."

"She says she needs an ambulance."

"Who is she?"

I can't describe how impossible it is to pronounce the name Harriet to a hidden audience. When you say it, you need to deal on the spot with the listener's reactions. To call a child Harriet is to condemn her to mediocrity.

My silence served me well. Roger, whose voice came closer, said, "Don't stand there rapping. If she's alone, let her in."

The door opened wider, and I felt a draft of cool air. So the dump did feature air conditioning. Leave it to Claude to rent me the sweat box. Behind Susan Hayward a bonfire glowed, the effect created by a red light bulb hanging like a jewel from the center of the ceiling. Roger, stripped to the waist, wearing nothing but Levi's held to his hips by a wide, silver, buckled belt, came forward with the grace of a god stepping out of the flames to welcome me into a new universe.

Even before I was privileged to partake of his exceptional personality, I recognized in Roger a soulmate, not to say a savior, which is unusual when you consider this childish prejudice I used to have regarding prematurely balding, soft-skinned, pale-eyed, fetus types; no, what I had was an unrehearsed revelation, an instantaneous appreciation of Roger's highly evolved inner state. Of course, at the time, I was too sick to realize it.

He double-checked the hall and, when he'd satisfied himself that I wasn't backed up by an army of Fuller

Brush men, let me in. I stood mutely while all the locks and chains on the door were rebolted.

My room could have easily fit into one corner of what had to be the Royal Suite. There were three heavily draped windows, one of them the proud container of a softly humming air conditioner. I saw armchairs, tables, a kitchen unit, rugs, and in the far corner, I could hardly credit my eyes, a huge, old-fashioned television set, the sound turned off, the blue-gray tube a bright haze of spinning, zigzag, dismembered lines. Two low sofa beds, pulled out from the wall, were angled at the unfocused tube. Try the horizontal knob, I almost shouted, my grave condition aggravated by the painful sight. I can't explain, but it was like watching an old friend writhing in agony.

There was a body sprawled on one of the beds, and Susan Hayward went and sat beside it, without bothering to adjust the set. The spacious room had a very lived-in, personal atmosphere, and I decided that Roger must be a permanent resident in the hotel. I was so busy taking inventory that I didn't realize that my host was speaking to me. Roger's voice is the original iron fist in the velvet glove, meaning that it is super soft but magnetically compelling. It may take a small effort to hear Roger's inaudible speech, but in the end one is rewarded with such wisdom that I say, give me one of Roger's inaudible sentences to all your collected works of William Shakespeare.

"What?" I said.

"I asked you, what's your problem?"

"I can't tell without the sound or picture."

"Your problem. You were making a racket about needing a doctor."

"Do you mind if I sit down?" I inquired, because I have a real phobia about standing around trying to explain myself.

"Watch, Roger," the pervert called from the TV corner. "It's just like going through the Holland Tunnel."

He ignored her and guided me around a naked girl, lying flat on her back, to a large maple armchair. "Sit here," he said. Mine was not to wonder why. I gratefully sank on the low cushions and proceeded to fall into a faint. Down down into the void I descended, head first. I was naturally horrified to be fainting in the midst of strangers. I observe the social niceties to the point of absurdity. You know the old wives' tale about how the hanged man's life flashes before his eyes? I felt as though I had sufficient time to recall in depth every single person who had failed me, while being swallowed into the abyss. That's when I realized it was no simple swoon but Super Pig closing my account.

"I'm dying," I cried and felt myself yanked forward by Roger's powerful grasp. My impression of Roger will indelibly remain that of the gallant hero who snatched me out of the lion's jaws, even though it developed that my awful descent was nothing more than me tipping backward in a recliner. Admittedly, the opulent furnishings should have prepared me for the luxury of a recliner. However, due to my European sojourn, I don't expect an oversized armchair with mismatched cushions to turn into a roller coaster.

148

Roger held my shaking hands in his firm grip. "What's happening, baby? You're white as a sheet." He sounded worried. "Are you on anything?"

"It seems," I said, when I'd regained my composure and with it the immediate obligation to relieve Roger's guilt regarding his social lapse, "that I'm on a seesaw, but I'm okay now."

"Henny Penny, get her a glass of wine."

"Roger, you haven't finished me," the naked girl on the floor murmured.

"I told you to get her a glass of wine."

"Oh, nuts," the girl cursed softly, lugging herself off the rug. She seemed afraid to refuse him. She padded on bare feet to a long wooden table, replica of the monstrosity in my tiny cell, and dutifully carted a glass of red wine to me. She hardly raised her eyes to Roger.

"Are you going to finish me?"

"Is that a question? Are you questioning me?"

The girl's neck got buried under her chin. "Lie down on the floor," he added kindly. "I just want to make our guest comfortable."

"Oh, thank you, Roger," she said jubilantly, clasping her hands in the beginning of a childish clap. She was down on her back in a flash.

The low, monotonous bongo playing resumed. I would have welcomed an introduction to the musician.

"Drink," Roger urged me. He released my hands. "Drink up and try to relax." A small sob, for which I was totally unprepared, rose out of my tight chest. He watched me closely, which made swallowing the bitter potion no easy matter.

"Better?"

It was neither the time nor the place to send back the bottle.

"Much." I thanked him. As Socrates remarked on the hemlock, It's the intention that counts.

"Relax," he repeated and gave my thigh a friendly squeeze.

The "ouch" sprang out of me as though I were a mechanical doll.

"Wow," he said. "What tension. You're a mess. It's fantastic."

I didn't know if I should feel insulted or flattered at his conflicting enthusiasms, so I sat stiffly at the edge of the treacherous chair, recovering my customary poise. As I regained my calm, my conscientious mind went back on the job. Who was Henny Penny? What was he going to finish doing to her? Who was the couple on the couch? Who was Roger? And who in that darkened room was wishing me dead, due to Roger's obsessive attentions?

"Lean back, but slowly this time." He smiled.

Let me get the business of Roger's teeth out of the way. They are the scars, the wounds of battles fought and won. They are the worn hieroglyphics of vulnerability. They tell you that this extraordinarily evolved man has known pain. I love Roger's bad teeth. While staring at Roger's teeth, as yet unaware that I was falling in love with them, I received an urgent message from my inner answering service. In essence the message was that if I tilted back, I would drop dead.

Senseless as these threatening calls are, they demand absolute obedience or a willingness to face the consequences. Since the tariff is always so high, death or madness or paralysis if I think certain words or look at the sky or eat a particular food, whatever, I've never put the terrorist threats to the test and by cooperating have managed to stay relatively alive.

"In a minute," I promised. Roger seemed to understand my predicament as though he had a wiretap inside my head.

"Take your time," he said in that hushed voice, as though it hurt his teeth to talk.

"Here, Roger." A familiar figure disentangled herself from the bongo player and moved toward us, a scarecrow in a fluttery negligee. She held a lit joint in her long, bony fingers, carried as far from her stick body as her stick arms would allow. It was as if she were transporting dirty socks or an equally choice tidbit. Her face was marked by what I instantly spotted as a perpetual sneer.

"Take a toke, darling."

She clearly had appointed herself the sole proprietor of all the men in the room, if not the world. Hadn't that very same sneer tried to intimidate me into buying a cheap hypoallergenic eye liner so I could look as embalmed as she?

"Haven't I seen you modeling on television?" I blurted and was answered by her sneer twisting into a positive paroxysm of disgust. I would gladly have donated my tongue to Hebrew National. Along with looking as though she needed to throw up, she sucked in her severely sunken cheeks and passed the joint to Roger.

"I'm wrecked," she bragged, as though it took a special talent to get stoned. Lord, spare me these dimpled darlings who are always congratulating themselves for not having any thoughts or feelings.

Roger accepted the offering, saying, "Thanks, Clarissa," and inhaled with a casual expertise that informed me he was no amateur freak. Holding his breath, he gestured the joint to me, but I refused with a decisive nod.

Of course I was tempted by its succulent aroma, but the truth is, I'm not so self-destructive as to turn on in a room with two hostile females, either one of whom could be my mortal enemy. Under such negative conditions, my powerful mind is likely to turn on me. I've learned to protect myself, meaning I get high with equals, men who can accompany the fantastic flights of my free-falling mind, not, I repeat, with a lackey such as Claude, whose only concern is whether you're being charming.

Naturally I worried lest Roger interpret my refusal as a personal rejection. Nothing could be further from the truth. If drugs gave him the courage to relate to me, then I could only support his readiness to grab at any straw. Being an instinctive psychologist, I concluded that Roger gained confidence by serving my needs. Parallel with that insight was the discovery that I'd forgotten my Marlboros, due to my recent bout of heart failure. No sooner did I become aware of my oversight than I experienced severe withdrawal symptoms.

"I'd love a Marlboro. I'm afraid I left mine in my room, but any filtered brand will do."

"Naughty, naughty," Clarissa sang. "Roger doesn't approve of commercial cigarettes. He thinks they're a nasty habit, don't you, Roger darling?"

Permit me to pause and reflect on my eternal enemy, female jealousy. As its number-one victim, I wish to go on record regarding female envy. It is the most destructive form of flattery ever invented. Its slings and arrows have caused me such trouble, I've sometimes wished myself invisible just to be rid of its tyranny. Go try to explain to a horde of furious women that my life, in spite of all appearances, isn't perfect.

"Roger is exceptionally lucky to have you do his listening and talking," I complimented her. "You're like a seeing-eye mouth."

"Roger, you promised," a voice at our heels wailed.

"Are you still down there, Henny Penny? For God's sake, get up."

"But you didn't finish me."

"Are you arguing with me?"

She jumped up, her face hidden by her drooping hair.

"Get dressed like a good girl."

"Yes, Roger." She scampered away like a child avoiding punishment.

"What room are you in?" he asked me in another voice.

"Just across the hall, 228."

153

"Is it locked? You heard, Henny Penny. Get her cigarettes, and fast."

"I think they're on the bed," I started to say.

"She'll find them. Anything else you need?"

I shook my head, a trifle unnerved by Roger's reversible moods. Henny Penny in an Indian shirt that barely reached her thighs was already at the door.

"Thank you," I called after her.

"Oh, Henny Penny is a great help. I couldn't cut it without her."

The girl took a second to smile at him before dashing on her errand.

Clarissa laughed. "Oh, darling, you'd make another Henny Penny."

"I love Henny Penny," Roger insisted. "She's a part of me."

"A mighty serviceable part, I must say."

"Essential. That's why she knows I'm completely hers."

It occurred to me that I had misread the situation or, at least, not read to the bottom of the page.

"Sweetie, you're absolutely my favorite couple," Clarissa crooned, confirming my worst fears. My heart sank at my neglect of Henny Penny, caused by my deficiency at making chitchat with a naked doormat.

The object in question came trotting in with the cigarettes, and while Roger graciously offered me a light, I tried to make contact with her. Forget it. I've looked into a few expressionless faces in my time, but beside Henny Penny's they become silent-screen stars'. Big, round, gray, unblinking, luminescent eyes were the only evidence that the machine was plugged in. She had round eyes in a round face on a round head, all held together by a skimpy brown ponytail. Well, whatever Roger was, he was no sucker for a pretty face.

The bongo player called out, "Penelope, bring me a cigarette."

Her unblinking eyes went first to Roger, and that communication accomplished, she jogged off into the shadowy corner, holding a single cigarette.

"She's a lovely girl," I said, because my silence felt rude.

"Enchanting," Clarissa mimicked me. "I'd better go protect my property." And with that the jealous harridan followed Henny Penny into the shadows.

Roger pulled a straight-back chair up close to mine. "Let's talk," he said, swiveling my recliner around so that my back was to the TV corner. From behind me I heard the melodious theme of the Late Late Show.

"Oh, fuck," Clarissa said, "*The Glen Miller Story* again."

Why doesn't she go home? I almost said out loud, but instead gave Roger my attention. The closer he got to me, the more I felt the intensity of his powerful personality.

He gave me his devastated smile. "Let's start real easy. What's your name?"

To some, particularly to some with names like Benton or Prentice, that might seem a simple enough question, but to me, it was a hole that I might or might not crawl out of. I paused.

"Okay," he said smoothly. "Be the mystery guest. I

like girls who don't blurt out their whole story. But we have to call you something. Suppose I give you a name."

"That depends," I responded cautiously. The fact is, I was afraid that what with our almost eerie rapport, he'd come up with Harriet.

"I see you as foreign." He felt for my identity with the sensitivity of a blind man fingering a Braille bible. "Secretive, artistic, sensual, and highly intuitive."

Would that my own mother had foreseen my temperament with such uncanny precision.

"I'm also highly intelligent," I confessed.

"Baby," Roger murmured in a tender moan, and I realized once and for all that with him the obvious would never need to be made explicit. A radiation of relief spread throughout my body. I knew that I was unthawing from my six frozen months with Claude. Roger put his hand on the front of my neck and squeezed his thumb against the pulse beating in my throat. This produced such a havoc of heat in my arms and chest that I became frightened of defrosting prematurely. Of melting into a shapeless blob on the comfortable recliner.

"Watch it with the hands," I said sharply.

"Yes," he said gently, removing the offending member. "It's been too long since you were touched with any skill or love. That's the sickness that brought you to my door, Leela."

"Who's Leela?"

"Leela is ancient Indian for God's play."

"I don't like it," I said flatly.

Roger shrugged.

"It's a bit too ancient."

"You're absolutely right. You're a child of our time. Don't worry it," he advised me. "The right name will come."

"What was this sickness of Leela's that you referred to?"

Roger appeared momentarily overcome. He put one hand over his pale eyes and raised the other in the air, snapping his fingers. Henny Penny rushed up to us, stuck a joint in Roger's lifted hand, and as promptly left us undisturbed.

Roger calmly lit the joint, inhaled, and offered it to me with a silent insistence. I just didn't have it in me to issue one more refusal. A look of satisfaction spread over Roger's bland face, telling me what I already knew: that he longed for us to be joined in all things.

We sat quietly passing the joint back and forth, except I had two or three puffs to Roger's one.

"Don't be afraid. It will help us to cut through the bullshit."

I felt its benefits almost immediately, what with the wine and the not eating.

"What are you doing?" I asked, because Roger had bent down and I heard a distinct mechanical click.

"It's nothing, baby."

"Let me decide." I leaned over to see what was happening.

"It's a tape recorder," he admitted.

I didn't like it. "Listen, are you a cop or something?" Let's face it, the police force had been in on my last three changes of address.

"Why would the cops be interested in you?"

That he would imagine me vulnerable to such trickery almost caused me to stand up and march out of the room. A flash image of the empty, stultifying cell across the hall convinced me to give him a second chance.

"Turn that thing off," I said, lighting a regular cigarette. The F.B.I. were welcome to a mile of tapes of Harriet blowing smoke rings.

"You're tough," Roger said and did as he was told.

It was our first disagreement, and I knew from the rush of angry tears how much I had been hurt. Roger reached out and took my free hand. He placed his thumb in the palm of my hand and pressed until I felt this dull ache that seemed to travel into my heart. It was as if he were opening my heart so that I could listen to him and not to the objections of my tired brain. I looked up and found him studying me.

"What are you doing?" I asked, because I sensed that he was doing something remarkable.

"I'm asking your body to trust me."

"That's a weird thing to do."

"Believe me, little girl, if you would learn to listen to the wisdom of your body, you would instantly know everything about me and I think you'd trust me. You'd know that I love you, and your struggle to guard yourself from me and the rest of the world would end. Give the victory to your body. Call a halt to the battle of questions and answers, and you'll know everything."

My body, captured by his thumb, responded, but my shell-shocked mind fought on.

I protested. "My body is just as opposed as the rest of me to a sneaky tape recording of a private conversation. Unlike other bodies you may have met lately, my body knows a rat when it smells one."

"You're too much." He released my hand and smiled his damaged smile.

I carefully placed my hand in my lap, afraid to leave it on its own. It seemed to be rebelling. Left to its own devices, my hand threatened to crawl back to Roger and make a separate peace. My heart closed with a disappointed thud, and I felt my body shake me.

"You're not angry at me?" I said, seized by this idiotic impulse to apologize.

"Angry?" he answered in astonishment, as if that word had no place in our shared vocabulary. "Baby, I'm impressed with you. I could tell that you had a special sense of yourself, a private brand of self-preservation. It's a miracle to come across a girl like you alone in this hotel. You are alone, aren't you?"

I nodded quickly, so as not to interrupt the outpourings of his bottled-up feelings.

"I ask myself, why would a beautiful girl like you be alone? There's only one possibility. You haven't given in. You haven't compromised because you can't compromise."

"Why can't I compromise?" I breathlessly asked.

"There are no compromises for your kind, baby. You're in a life-and-death struggle. When you open up to someone, you open all the way. You hold nothing back. You need a strong man, not the weaklings, the uptight specimens this society calls men. And I doubt if you've found him yet. Once you find him, it will be for always. You'll pour your life into him. You'll be two loving bodies serving one mind. You can't risk pouring that river of love into the wrong man. For a woman of your intensity to open herself to an ordinary man would be worse than suicide or murder. You haven't murdered anyone, have you?" he jested with me.

"No." I laughed. "But I've been tempted."

"I'm hip," he said, pulling in the reins of his excitement. I waited for him to continue, but he just sat there sternly, lost in his own complex thoughts.

"I've tried to compromise," I timidly admitted. "Frequently."

He unconsciously placed his hands on the back of my neck under my hair and kneaded my shoulders. I felt my face flush, and an uncontrollable shudder shook my head.

"It's awful, awful. The terrible isolation of integrity."

"No, sweet baby," he put his mouth against my ear. "I'm not angry at you."

His hand went up my neck, his strong fingers massaging the base of my skull, and incredibly, my throat and chest became choked with a scream. It was as though he had found the hidden spring that opened the Chinese box.

"Let go," he urged me, but I didn't dare and strangled the sound. Only now I knew, as though I had heard it, the solid mass of sound that was lodged inside of me. I didn't feel frightened of Roger, who couldn't imagine the effects of what he was doing, but of myself. I wanted desperately to feel normal again. No sooner had I wished the wish than I noticed I was paralyzed from the waist down.

"I can't walk," I cried, which was a strange announcement to make, considering I was sitting in a chair.

"Christ." Roger pulled away from me. "Look at you. You're tied up like the Man of Rubber. Here." He straightened my legs, which were braided under my full weight, and briskly rubbed the rigor mortis out of them. He laid my legs across his lap, my bare feet dangling out of my bell-bottoms. I lit another cigarette to avoid having to look at Roger.

"Comfortable?" he asked, absentmindedly playing with the soles of my feet.

"That tickles," I lied, because why tell him it felt as though buckets of warm water were pouring down the insides of my thighs?

"You're just a bundle of beautiful nerves," he told me. "Beautiful, starved nerves."

"How come you know so much about me?" I shyly asked, since I was becoming increasingly aware of his perfect batting average.

"Maybe it's because I've been studying you all my life," he answered with a tight-lipped smile, which was my favorite smile thus far.

"That's silly. We just met, remember?"

"Did we, or have we met over and over again in the wrong places at the wrong time? Haven't we met but not been ready for each other?"

I personally feel I was born ready, but you can't keep correcting genuine effort.

He wove his fingers between my toes as if he were clasping a beloved hand. "Haven't we worked to perfect ourselves for this meeting?"

"I don't know," I said stupidly, since I suddenly found myself doing my thinking in my toes.

"You're right," he corrected himself with his uncanny precision. "Women are more complete than men. You're born with perfect knowledge. Men are given the keys, but women contain the treasures. For men to become truly men, we must first attain the female side of our nature. Then we can hope to reach your treasures. Men must work while women wait."

"That's more like it," I agreed.

"But how many women despair? How many countless women try to do the work men must do for themselves and, in the end, bury their treasures?"

"Most, I would say."

"But those few who haven't, those isolated few." He pressed my foot between his hands as if in prayer, gallantly refraining from naming names. "Those few survivors wait, in perfect patience."

"I've occasionally become impatient," I confessed.

"Not really, or you wouldn't be the person I see in front of me, a miraculously untouched woman."

I took Roger far too seriously to come sailing into his life under false colors.

"You know, until yesterday I was living with a man. A French movie director. I left him."

"Is that right?"

"Yes. A highly regarded director. He had all the trappings of a real man, wealth, refinement, good looks."

I couldn't help but wonder if that sniveling rat Claude would ever describe me in such generous terms.

"It was terrible. He loved me, or at least he thought he loved me. I suppose these men who haven't, as you say, done their homework are capable of some degree of love. But such a tyrannical love, words fail me. If I went shopping, he imagined the grocer was panting after me in the streets. If we went to a lousy movie, he thought everyone in the audience was watching me, not the screen. Did you by any chance see an Italian movie about Christ and his fag cronies?"

Roger, his attention unashamedly riveted on me, said no.

"Oh well, it doesn't really matter. You saved yourself a buck. It got to a point where my boy friend became jealous of me even talking to a woman, if you can imagine. I was expected to sit next to him in restaurants like the Sphinx. He finally dragged one of these women home, and believe me she was your typical buried treasure. Dragged her into our home that I personally cooked and cleaned in, to prove that one: she was after him not me, which I strongly doubt, key or no key, and two: I'd better pay undivided attention to his selfish sexual proclivities. My God, when I think of his sexual peculiarities! I began to feel more like an industry than a woman."

Roger sat so gravely, I was afraid he might be measuring his own worth against that of the debonair lover I had inadvertently described. But was I expected to conceal my true identity forever? In a way you couldn't imagine Roger in a restaurant, no less behind a megaphone ordering stars around. Maybe in a shirt and tie or a turtleneck sweater, but not with that bare, sparsely haired, gleaming white chest. I impulsively put my hand on Roger's soft chest and stroked him, as if I would stroke his pain away.

He grabbed my hand and held it pressed against him. "Oh, you touched me."

I wanted to assure him that I'd touched much worse, but on the heels of my painful confessions, that smacked of cold comfort.

What I did say was, "Roger, I promise you if Claude broke into this room this instant and fell down on his knees in front of me . . ." But that was a promise I was not obliged to finish. Speak of coincidences. No sooner were those prophetic words out of my mouth than we all heard a tapping on the door.

"Who the hell is that?" Roger pulled my hand off his chest as if it were a branding iron.

"Oh, Roger," Clarissa's voice drifted over from the TV party, "it must be Libby. Remember, Daddy, you sent for her?"

"Right. I forgot all about her. Make sure it's her, Clarissa, before you open up."

Roger jabbed a finger at me. "You keep your mouth shut. Not a word, understand? You're an Albanian. You don't speak American. Dig?"

"Sure, Roger," I said, calculating the penance he'd

have to undergo for using such an abusive tone of voice.

"Okay, let them in. I want everyone to cool it. Aaron, no more bongos. Turn the sound down, Henny Penny."

On second thought Roger did have the makings of a movie director. His final touch in setting the scene was to switch on the tape recorder.

10

*I*N SPITE of the Albanian ban placed on me, it felt sweet to be on the inside. Clarissa ushered a couple into the room. They stood close together, hands clasped, like Hansel and Gretel facing the wicked witch.

"Hi," Roger greeted them. "I was afraid you wouldn't make it. Henny Penny, round up some chairs."

Henny Penny bustled about, chattering gaily as she dragged chairs to the table. "Hello, Libby. Roger and I came to New York especially to see you."

"Oh, Christ," Libby said. "You've still got that burned-out handmaiden in tow."

Roger, seated, reached behind him for the bottle of wine Henny Penny was holding. "Now, Libby, let's not start off on the wrong foot. This is a friendly get-together."

Henny Penny, no doubt encouraged by Roger's saintly patience, babbled on: "Victor has a new rule at the Institute. None of the girls is allowed to ask questions, not even to say how are you or what's new. It's so hard not to ask questions, especially when you're being punished and you want to know the reason." She giggled. "But it's so much fun. Victor says we mustn't even think questions, and I never do. Roger," she said studiously, "since Libby isn't at the Institute any more, could I ask her a question? Oh," she covered her mouth, "I asked a question. See what I mean, Libby? Oh," she squealed, "I did it again."

"Get back on the bed, Henny Penny, and be quiet. Don't bother Libby."

God knows what, if anything, her babbling was about. Roger, with his exquisite tact, made no further reference to what had to be a social embarrassment. "How come so late? I've been here all day."

"I waited till Bryant got home," Libby answered in a small voice.

"What are you up to, Bryant?"

"I'm pushing a cab," the boy answered, with a narrow-shouldered shrug. "It's not a bad gig."

Clarissa sidled up to the conference table and poured herself a glass of wine.

"Thanks for giving Roger our address," Libby said with a quiet bitterness. "It saved us the trouble of writing to him."

Clarissa lifted her glass in a welcoming toast. "It was nothing. I knew you'd be totally dragged if Roger passed through town and you missed him. Why, when he called and said he was dying to see you, I insisted that we have the grand reunion here."

My first horrible realization that I was squatting on Clarissa's property hit me like an injection of horror serum. It was not Roger's room, it was hers. My chin went haywire. The idea of dashing over to borrow a cup of sugar from the shrew, or stopping in for a convivial television night, or most remote of all, having a philosophical exchange such as I had been enjoying with Roger was so grotesque that I shot out of her rickety recliner and spilled the sour wine all over my white jeans.

"Who's she?" Libby rudely demanded, turning her charity poster eyes on me. The couple, adorned in his-and-her, cut-down, faded dungarees and Elvis Presley sweat shirts, both extremely thin and dark and fatigued, looked as if they had stepped out of a CARE commercial. GIVE, they seemed to shout, HELP. They were a fund raiser's dream come true.

Roger tried gallantly to shield me. "Oh, she's nobody, Libby. She's a chick from across the hall. Doesn't speak a word of English."

"I bet," she said and gave me the typical hostile stare that welfare cases bestow on potential benefactors. I myself did not wish to contribute to her cause.

"I happen to be an Albanian refugee!"

"Sit down, stupid," Roger snapped, and since everyone else was seated, I had to assume the incredible reference was to myself.

"A new candidate for the Institute? Where do you find them, Roger?"

Clarissa, who persisted in this loathsome tendency to answer for Roger, stuck her two cents in. "This one found him, I swear. She swam to the door like a lemming."

No, dear neighbor, I meditated, friendship is not in the books for us.

Roger slumped down in his chair, his hands folded behind his head.

"Funny, I was just thinking of the day you came to the door of the Institute, begging to be admitted. Remember, Libby? You were freaking out. Suicide threats galore if Victor didn't take you in. How you begged him. How you promised to love, honor, and obey. You were beautiful. Remember, Bryant? And Victor, who has never failed you, who loves you, found a place for you at his table. Didn't he, Libby?"

"I guess so," she said faintly, and then with more energy, "But I was crazy."

"Victor was aware of that. Everyone was, with the possible exception of Bryant here, who sees only what he wants to see. The Institute never could turn you into a man, Bryant, but that's cool. Society needs its cab drivers. If a man has the soul of a flunky, then there's really no place for him in the Institute."

They took his insult quietly. Only Clarissa broke in, laughing her snide laugh. "You're such a terrible snob, Roger."

"That's right. Victor taught me to put a high price on my time and on my company."

"Victor," Clarissa said with disdain. "I knew him when he landed in town, trotting around, carrying anyone's guitar case. Of course, that was before he discovered he was God."

At long last Roger had it with the harpy. "Shut up, Clarissa. We all know you're old."

"But Victor is God," Henny Penny protested. "Once I saw him float. Oh, it looked like so much fun."

"Did I tell you to be quiet!" I suddenly had this vision of poor Roger in a cage filled with snarling females. He flicked the whip at Libby.

"Did Victor turn you away for being crazy? Or did he take you into his heart and into his family?"

"It wasn't like that," Libby said and started to cry.

"Why wasn't it like that?"

"I don't know. I don't understand him." The words came out in shudders. "I don't understand any of it. I just know Victor likes flips around him. He keeps talking about love and no one ever notices what a creep he is. He's a creep. Everyone near him gets sick or dies. Why doesn't he die?" she howled.

After that outburst, a thick silence crept over the room of a variety that used to provoke my ailing mother to claim she could hear her blood pressure drop.

"Your ingratitude wounds me, baby. Here you are, recovered enough to fight with me, which really makes me proud of you, though I wish you were fighting your enemies, not your friends. Your head is together, you've got a man at your side, all supplied by the Institute, though the purpose of the Institute is not to act as a mating service, and you're saying you want Victor dead? Why, if not for Victor, you'd be dead, and you're not the only Libby in this world."

"I didn't really mean it that way," she said softly.

"She really didn't mean it, Roger," Bryant hastily added. "She's just very upset. Get hold of yourself, Libby."

I was beginning to get the picture. She was one of these professional helpless types. A smaller, younger version of the Rhoda-Reginas, who throw themselves on your mercy and then hate you for whatever help you give. Why? Because you can never give them enough. *More* is the only word in their dictionaries. And when there is no more, when they've completely drained you, then guess who gets to play villain? I wanted to rush to Roger and warn him not to waste his rational words on her or he'd end up believing he was the crazy one. I longed to tell him about Rhoda-Regina and the thanks I'd gotten from her. Happily, I detected a bit more steel in Roger's hushed voice.

"I'm going to give you an opportunity to repay Victor for all the good he's done you, and I hope you'll grab it, Libby. Victor is worried. He's worried because one of his Libbys has strayed from the flock. He made an exception when he let you and Bryant go, and Victor often talks about it, questions himself about it. Did he do the right thing? Convince him he did the right thing. Help him to find his lost little girl. Help him to find Heidi. Where is she?"

"I don't know," Libby moaned.

Roger pretended he hadn't heard her. "Victor thinks you know where she is because he found a letter from you that Heidi, despite all rules, managed to receive."

"Oh," said Libby faintly.

Bryant got plugged in. "Tell him. Cut this crap out.

You know how they can fuck up our scene, and for what? If Victor wants Heidi, he'll get her. Tell him and let's get the fuck out of here."

"For once he's right, Libby. The way Victor figures it, there are no accidents, no mistakes. Heidi left that letter because she wants to be found. She needs to be found. She knows Victor loves her, and she's a part of him."

"I can't fink on her." Libby wept. "He'll kill her. What does he want her for? He's not hot for her. He doesn't fuck her. He's not hot for anyone. It's all a shitty ego trip."

Roger put his hand on Libby's arm, and she swallowed hard. "It's not up to you, Libby, to stick your nose into Victor's private affairs. How Victor loves is Victor's trip. We won't talk about it. It won't come up again in our discussion, right? Victor figures that Heidi got confused. Maybe you convinced her she wasn't loved? Anyway, she's made her point. She wanted proof of Victor's love. She wanted Victor to follow her, and he's following. You know what I think?" he said with delayed male inspiration, because I myself had been thinking it since Heidi's name had turned up, "I think that you're standing between them. Let's assume Heidi managed to smuggle out a few complaints to you. Don't women always complain about their old man? Isn't that their trip? So you pump Heidi full of this notion of splitting on Victor, and she does. Now you're determined to turn a girlish prank, a stupid impulse, into a permanent break. It must have bugged you, baby, when Victor preferred Heidi and you had to settle for this loser. I'll never understand how you chicks keep doing this number on each other."

"Shit," Libby said, and then, "Heidi has as much right to live as Victor. He turned her into a vegetable. You saw. I think he hates her. He always hated her because she had spirit, even if she was a complete flip. She was funny. Please, Roger, don't ask me to fink on her. I couldn't stand myself. Listen, I have an idea. Why don't you tell Victor you couldn't find me. Take her," she said pointing at me. "Give him someone new to break in, to discipline. She's older than Heidi, but I don't think Victor cares about things like that. Please, Roger."

"No, she's too old and fat." If that slander had come from any source other than Henny Penny, I would have stuck an Albanian knife into its heart.

With that outrageous suggestion, Libby lost Roger and blew the game. She had overlooked the limits of his John Alden number. I was that limit. Due to her obsessive inability to grant other women the smallest degree of importance, referring to us as vegetables, the highest form of flattery being that we were "funny," she had refused to take notice of Roger's well-concealed infatuation with me and, with that spectacular blunder, had alienated Roger.

Roger, tense and hurt, slipped a sheet of white paper across the table. "I'm going to make it easy for you, Libby. Some things are hard to say, easier to write, if that letter you sent to Heidi is any indication of how you operate. Write down her address, and make it fast."

Libby, unable to concede defeat, sat motionless over the paper. It was Bryant who finally had his fill of her obstinacy. He grabbed the paper and wrote quickly.

"Come on," he said to her, and they both stood up. Roger, still seated, read, "Montreal." He whistled. "Of course, she's crashing with Leon."

"You'll never get her back, never. Leon's father is a big shot, a senator or a governor. He'll protect Heidi."

"That's not your problem; you did your best and that Victor will appreciate." He followed them to the door, continuing to demonstrate his exceptional let-by-gones-be-bygones nature, which was so akin to my own.

Standing between them, he draped his arms loosely over their shoulders. "Remember, Victor loves you, both of you, and any time you want back into the Institute, there'll always be a place for you at his table."

Libby fumbled with the locks and managed to get the door open. "I hate all of you," she shouted, with her back to us. But I wasn't paying the slightest attention to her. I was calculating how little space an Albanian person such as myself would take at Victor's table.

Roger bolted the door after them and came spinning into the center of the room. "Montreal." He laughed out loud. "Today Montreal, tomorrow the world."

"I don't know how you managed to scare the information out of her," Clarissa droned in her monotone. I now knew, with a terrible stab at my heart, why Roger tolerated her presence. He grabbed his hostess and spun her around.

"It's because we're powerful, my love." He beat a

Tarzan tom-tom on his bare chest. "We are powerful. Victor will break Leon's ass," he said with delight. "We've got his kid sister up there, freaked but good. She's on a Mary Magdalene trip. Her idea of salvation is to wash Victor's feet. Wow," Roger said, rubbing his hands together, "I wonder if it's too late to call Victor?"

"He never used to sleep," Clarissa said.

"Yes, but he gets into other things. I'd better wait till tomorrow."

"Are we going to Montreal?" Henny Penny asked.

"That's a long drive, man," the musician joined in.

"It won't be too bad. I'll break it. Drop off Henny Penny at the Institute and pick up additional troops, if Victor thinks we have to use force."

"But I want to go to Montreal with you," Henny Penny complained, and I thought for a dreadful second that my words had issued from her dummy mouth. I had this awful premonition of Roger walking out of my life without ever knowing what he meant to me. I suffered the cruel pressure of time colliding with my absurd timidity. When would I be free of my prim restraint? If only I could be a Rhoda-Regina or a Maxine for one minute, express my needs, insist on them, let the bodies fall where they may. But no. There were certain inescapable laws in my upbringing, and number one on the forbidden list was to express feelings of attachment or affection too soon. To the man must fall the illusion of the successful pursuit. I knew, from bitter experience, that women were masters of a subtle form of encouragement. They somehow managed to capture the bungling hunter, while creating precisely the opposite impression. That know-how my mother had cunningly withheld from me. In truth, I was burdened with a male mentality. I wanted to grab Roger, fling him on my horse, and be abducted. I was too tired. It was too late for me to start learning feminine wiles. I did not know how to reverse the roles that I am sure nature intended us to reverse. Me with my inscrutable passions. I needed a man to shoot himself before I acknowledged that he was alive. I grabbed my head in my two hands to hold it steady.

Roger came waltzing over to me. "Did anyone ever tell you that you make a gorgeous Albanian?"

"No."

"What's the matter? Why are you holding your head like that? Are you feeling sick again?" He leaned over me and caressed the top of my head, triggering off a hail of shivers that rained down my neck and back. I almost cried out to him, "Roger, you win," but no, I had to pull a Doris Day and push his hand away.

"Hey," Roger said, lowering himself to the arm of the recliner, "are you mad at me?"

"You called me stupid," I said stupidly.

He couldn't balance himself on the precarious tilting arm and sat down on the floor in front of me, resting his head on my knees. I would have appreciated a few additional strands of hair to run my fingers through. For a change, life had given me an impossible scene to play.

"Oh, baby, I'm sorry. You mustn't be so paranoid. I just wanted to get that bad business about Heidi out of the way. You know I love you?"

How easy it is for a man to speak his piece. If I said I love you back, he'd probably have a stroke. How could I respond to Roger without endangering his health? My mind had never been blanker. Nothing. Not a glimmer, not a trace of thought. Empty. I hate that sensation of all the fuses blowing; there was Roger, at my feet, yearning for rapport.

I almost welcomed Clarissa's insensitive intrusion. I could hear her clicking the channel dial.

"Balls," she said. "Nothing but June Allyson being brave," and then, giggling, "Oh my, Henny Penny's at it again."

"Don't bug her," Roger advised. "It will get her to sleep."

"It ain't helping me to sleep," the musician said.

I felt somehow that he was the only other kindred soul in the room.

"Leave it alone, Clarissa. Come here, you witch." There were rustles and grunts from the TV corner and then the sounds of whispering. I wondered if Clarissa was hinting that I should leave. The word leave seemed to permeate the atmosphere. Roger was leaving. He was going to sacrifice our budding relationship and leave to chase after a spoiled brat who was sulking in Montreal. No one was driving across borders to rescue me, to deliver me into the arms of a worried lover.

"I envy Heidi," I said. What worlds I tried to communicate with that simple confession.

"You do?" Roger covered his delight with a mask of surprise.

"She's a lucky girl."

"Why?"

"To have you see through Libby's game, and persist, and go after her. I don't think there's anything more important than to be missed, wanted. Victor is lucky, too, to have a friend like you. Most people don't even want to know about anyone else's troubles, much less actually do something about it. But I'm like you. I swear. My friends' problems become as important as my own, more important. I just wanted you to know," I said, "that I admire what you're doing."

"That's beautiful." He embraced my knees. "There aren't many women who have your understanding."

"Oh, I know. I personally haven't met any. Take my so-called friend Rhoda-Regina, a mess, a catastrophe. I came back from Paris especially as the result of an intuition I had to help her. I lived in Paris most of my life," I added.

I felt obliged to exaggerate slightly, because we had so little time left, and if I revealed myself in five-year hunks it would take forever.

"I hope you'll never have cause to regret it, Roger. I hope that Victor doesn't turn on you the way my friend turned on me. But he sounds like an exceptional person, not a Rhoda-Regina, who is in no way exceptional, except for being exceptionally large and exceptionally stingy. I've frequently noticed that very large people, fat in fact, want it all for themselves." I was horrified to find myself squandering our brief moments analyzing Rhoda-Regina. There was so much I needed to know about Roger and the Institute and Victor. I put my hand on Roger's gleaming, bare shoulder.

Roger looked up at me with unconcealed admiration. "It must be tough for an exceptional woman like you to make it, out here, with the lame brains. God knows," he said pensively, "what lunatic asylum or prison I'd be in if I hadn't met Victor."

"He sounds like a wonderful fellow." I brushed Roger's skin with my fingertips.

"I'd kill for him," Roger said passionately. "Victor saved my life."

"Is he rich? How does he feed all these people he invites to his table? I mean, when you get invited to Rhoda-Regina's table, which is never, you're expected to bring your own sack of potatoes."

"He manages," he said vaguely. "Victor is a genius, a medicine man. Victor has powers. Whatever he needs, he gets. Victor is in touch."

"I see," I said. I certainly would have appreciated a less analytical answer. "And Victor takes care of everyone with his powers?"

"Of course. Victor is the spirit of the Institute. Our teacher. We share all our possessions, including our knowledge. We support each other in order to develop our full human potential."

Much as I respected Roger's elevated concepts, I wanted to be absolutely sure that we were talking the same language. "You mean nobody at the Institute has to work?"

"Are you kidding? You think self-realization isn't work? We're a school. Every minute of our day is dedicated to expanding self-knowledge and achieving ultimate consciousness."

"I mean, work for a living."

"Living is our work. We study ourselves, we study each other, we question our every move, we record and memorize all interactions in order to escape the past and live fully in the immediate moment."

"I see. How interesting. Do you do all this hard work in a big old sprawling farmhouse?"

"Not quite," he said reluctantly. "Last year we acquired a motel. . . Hey." He laughed nervously under my skillful touch.

"How fabulous," I exclaimed, thrilled to have a concrete description of the Institute. "I adore motels, all those color TV sets, and everything in the world a person needs practically built into the bed. Where is it located?"

"No more questions, baby, you're a bad girl to let me talk so much. You're such a groove to rap with, a soulmate," he said helplessly. "But Victor has a rule, we're not allowed to discuss the Institute with outsiders."

"Just tell me where it is," I persisted.

"Easy, baby, not so loud. We don't want to wake up the whole hotel. It's in Vermont," he admitted. "Enough about my scene. Let's pay some attention to you."

"Vermont! What a coincidence. That's my favorite state in America. I saw it in a Hitchcock movie. God, it was magnificent, stole the picture. The plot was about this bum who's buried there in the woods, and Shirley MacLaine, his wife, is looking for him, and she keeps tramping through the woods, and all you ever see are her dead husband's feet sticking out of this fabulous foliage. It takes place in the fall, which is in a couple of weeks, when you stop to think about it. Vermont will be on fire, glorious. I bet I could stop smoking in a place like Vermont. Here, I figure the less you breathe, the safer you are. And the Institute, smack in the middle of my favorite state. Lucky, lucky Heidi, not to be dragged back to a slum like Twenty-third Street. I myself would be ready on a minute's notice to leave this rat race and indulge my love of nature."

"Shhhh," Roger said. "People are trying to sleep. Come down here, baby, so we can talk without disturbing anyone."

"Down on the floor?"

"Come on." He pulled at my legs. "It will be relaxing for you to stretch out."

The activity in Clarissa's bed had exactly the same rhythm as the blood pumping in my ears.

"I'm really very relaxed, now that I've mastered this rocking horse." I laughed.

He tugged at me. "Doctor's orders." He patted the floor next to him. "Lie down."

I couldn't think of any objections I might raise that Roger wouldn't interpret as a personal insult, so I slipped off the chair and sat down beside him. He still wasn't satisfied.

"No, no. Lie down. You've been sitting up all night."

"Believe me, I'm used to it. Neither of my parents, both of whom are now dead, ever slept. Especially my mother. She offered a huge reward to anyone who could catch her sleeping, and if my memory serves me, no one ever collected."

"Hey, relax."

I stretched out, my eyes open, and found myself in a new universe of table legs and bottoms of beds; scattered there were records and magazines and empty bags and shoes and underwear.

"That's better." Roger sat beside me, with his legs crossed, his bare feet resting on his thighs. I could see the black soles of his feet as he gently played with his own toes.

"Sweet baby," he said, "sitting up like a good little girl all night and not one complaint. Does that feel good? Are you comfortable?"

"Yes, Roger," I said, and my eyes filled with tears. It felt too strange to talk, because I could hear the words vibrate in the back of my head, which was against the floor. The truth is my body hurt as if it were being broken on a medieval rack. Roger put his palm flat on my solar plexus and pressed.

I gasped with pain, because he had managed to find my sorest spot. All the aches in my arms and legs and heart seemed to radiate from that particular spot.

"Poor brave baby," Roger murmured, "how can you breathe with that knot blocking your chest? It's terrible, baby, you're barely alive. What can I do for you? I have so little time. Damn it." He seemed genuinely upset. "I knew you were in trouble, but this is murder. Turn over," he said in the same dreary voice. "Let me check your back."

I didn't even think of protesting. Roger adjusted my arms and hands so that they cushioned my face. He pressed a place between my shoulder blades that was directly connected to the disaster area he had located in my chest and I screamed.

"This is no good, baby. You're practically a cripple." Something decisive happened to his voice. "I can't allow it. I can't leave you in this condition. I must do something, just for the time being. It can't be much, but it will do some good till we can really fix you up." He worked his fingers down my spine, and at each step of his journey he set off bolts of electricity that searched my body for hidden sites of pain. His fingers got to the belt of my jeans and stopped.

"Turn around slowly, don't punish yourself any more than you need to. Right," he said and helped roll me over on my back.

"Take off your T shirt."

"What?"

He hardly looked at me. "I can't see what I'm doing with you stuffed into all those clothes."

"You mean you want me to get undressed?"

"That's exactly what I mean."

"But we're not alone," I blurted out, which wasn't at all what I meant. It was that I could hear Clarissa and the musician softly urging each other to greater and greater efforts, and their quick panting was becoming mixed in with my breathing, and though I trusted Roger and knew he wanted to serve me, I was trembling with confusion.

"Of course we're alone. Any time we're together, we'll always be alone." He rubbed the spot that had caused me such agony, and miraculously I felt the pain disappearing and in its place an expanding pool began to fill with soothing warmth.

"Oh, Roger, that feels so nice."

"I'm glad I'm not too late. You've been abused and neglected, dear child, but I think Daddy can make it better."

"Couldn't he do it through my shirt? I mean, that feels perfect."

How could I get through Roger's desire to heal me and communicate to him that though I appreciated what he was doing, we were not alone. We were only two in a world filled with degenerates.

Roger lifted his hand, and a hard sob shook out of me.

"I can't blame you. A lovely girl like you must have her trust violated so often that finally you don't dare trust any man. I'm sorry. I had no right to expect you to see me in another light. That's why I despise those faggots who hide their hate behind lust, force sweet girls like you to close up in self-defense. We get their victims at the Institute all the time. Girls who have been so wounded, so betrayed, we can't do anything to reach them. It's over. They're lost. Those are the hardest cases to send away, because I know the hell they're being sent back to. Poor babies, poor lost babies." He stroked my hair.

I tried to bargain. "If I take my clothes off, will you promise me I can get dressed any time I want? And you won't get hurt or angry?"

"Sweetheart, you mustn't do anything that you don't feel completely easy about. I want you to relax, baby, you're already at the breaking point. Don't force anything."

I had almost forgotten about Clarissa and the musician, until I heard them groaning each other's names, over and over again, and then, there was a wonderful safe silence in the room. Roger, with his sublime tact, left me. Thank God. My bra looked as though I had wiped tables with it, and my panties didn't exist. I put everything in a pile next to me and shoved my bra into a pocket. Roger came back into our circle of red light and arranged himself in his yoga position. Just as my trusting nature had anticipated, he was fully dressed. He held out a Pepperidge Farm bag to me and smiled his charming, ruined smile.

"Do you like chocolate-chip cookies?"

"Sure." I took a few, wondering what I had been so nervous about. "They're delicious." I discovered I was starving.

Roger lit a joint and inhaled deeply. "Will you promise not to get uptight if I tell you something?" He handed me the joint, which I accepted, but swallowed a minimum of smoke.

"What?" I said.

"You have an extremely beautiful body. A real mature woman's body. You're a feast, my love."

I couldn't be sure if it was the reflection of the light or if Roger's face was flushed. He brushed a sprinkling of crumbs off my chest and said in a thick voice, "Now

I want you to lie down on your back, close your eyes, and let yourself think your favorite thoughts. The ones that send you to sleep."

I did as I was told and was grateful to close my eyes so that Roger could not see into my thoughts, which were nothing less than a pornographic scenario starring me in my present position surrounded by a large cast of naked men with the most obscene intentions. In my private production I was blindfolded and probably tied down, as well as being a helpless captive; their wishes were my commands and none of them seemed to have the slightest respect for me. How different from Roger's gentle and careful manner. He ran his fingers lightly over my skin, hardly touching me, but I shivered and felt goose bumps rise like welts all over my body.

"My beautiful girl. Allow me to make one more personal observation, and then to work."

I allowed him.

"You have an incredible skin, a rare skin. So soft and iridescent in this light. Excuse me for sounding a bit dippy," he laughed nervously, "but it reminds me of the skins the Old Masters painted. Those angels who seem to be lit from the inside. My voluptuous angel," he bashfully mumbled. "Okay, enough of telling you what you already know. Now, let's get serious."

He took my hands and placed them, one on each breast.

"Just relax," he said. I felt his hands rotating over my stomach, not lightly, but with a deep touch that found and outlined my intestines.

186

It provoked the most alarming effect of opening and spreading the muscles that kept my body sealed, and I tightened my hold on my breasts as though that would keep my guts from spilling out.

Roger, with his uncanny insight, anticipated my panic.

"Relax, angel. Don't be afraid. It isn't going to happen. I won't let you lose control of your sweet body. The fear you're feeling, that your insides are going to rush out, is just your blood finally feeding those starved nerves down here."

He moved his hand down my pelvis. "Feel the blood pumping into your groin?"

"Yes, Roger."

"Spread your legs, angel, not too much, just enough that you don't interfere with your circulation." He carefully parted my legs. His fingers concentrated high on the inside of my thighs.

"You're terrific, angel. We have girls at the Institute who can't let their pelvis come to life. Do you feel warm streamings going up into your body?"

"Yes, Roger. Roger?"

"What, angel?"

"My name is Harriet."

"Harriet," he repeated. I had the rare pleasure of enjoying the sound of my name.

"Roger?"

"Yes, Harriet."

"When are you coming back for me?" It was the most natural thing to ask, lying there with my eyes tightly closed.

It must have been such a relief for him to finally hear those words that he couldn't answer. He tightened his grasp on my thighs.

I forgot to wait for his answer because I was suddenly terrified that all these streamings he had mentioned were going to stream out of me, pouring hot waves of juice over his busy hands. I gasped to hold back the flood.

"Good," he said, "perfect. I can hardly believe how swift, how full your responses are. Baby, you were born to give pleasure. Listen carefully. I want to teach you a few simple techniques you can do yourself, just until I get back. You have to learn to listen to your body, and to do that, you have to learn how to make it sing. Now take your nipples between three fingers, and very carefully, very slowly twist them, the way you would twist the petals off a bud."

I was too embarrassed, not so much because of Roger, whom I trusted, but because my naked gentlemen were crowding in for a better view. Roger misread my reluctance.

"Should I show you what to do?"

"Oh, no. I understand, I promise, I'll do that exercise alone, every day, while I wait for you to come for me."

"No, no, Harriet, I want to explain the benefits it has on the rest of your system, and for that, you must do it here, with me watching."

I shakily tried to comply.

"My wonderful, free baby." He moved his hands up and under my hips and, with a circular motion, kneaded some muscles I never knew I had. I could no longer be sure if he was hurting me.

"Ohhh," I said.

"I can't believe you, Harriet. You're too perfect. Those proud nipples standing up like they would feed the entire world. The nipples of a goddess." He laughed softly. "I always believed, even when I was a kid, that the apple Eve gave to Adam was her luscious tit, no more luscious than yours, my love, and once he tasted her fruit, he was insatiable, haunted. He could never get enough. I wonder, what man could ever have enough of you? Don't let me get off the track," he said severely, more to himself than to me.

"Now tell me, baby, do you feel your whole chest swelling?"

"Yes."

"Is your face flushing?"

"Yes."

"Do you feel as if your fingers are actually inside your body, inside your sweet pussy?"

"Yes," I said faintly.

"Fantastic. Now remember, the nipples stimulate and vitalize your entire nervous system, from head to toe. It's essential to your health that you keep those nerve paths functioning. Let me show you."

He took my hand and lightly placed it on my damp pubic hairs. In my concentration I'd forgotten that Roger was watching all of me, and I became rigid with the naked consciousness of myself. He kept his hand on top of mine and serenely ignored my prudish behavior. He pressed my finger into my wet body.

"Keep it up with the left nipple," he directed me. "Now, Harriet, I want you to observe how your body becomes one undifferentiated mass of feelings. It doesn't know any more where your fingers are located. It's beginning to free itself of its murderous fragmentation. It's becoming a unity, a simple, palpitating diffusion of sensations. Go ahead, play with it, confuse it, show it some love. My beautiful free brave girl, it makes me so happy to watch you make yourself happy."

"I shouldn't," I whimpered. My heart was pounding, and I was concerned that considerably more than Roger had counted on was occurring.

"You must. Listen to your body. Be kind to it. It deserves care and love. It's demanding love. Open your eyes, look at me, baby; let me see how happy you're making yourself, please."

I forced my eyes open and saw Roger's pale face gleaming over me. He sat like a remote, smiling statue, his hands clasping his knees. I saw that his eyes were bloodshot, the rims speckled with white flakes, his face drawn with a profound fatigue. He didn't move, but held my eyes trapped in his.

"Don't stop," the statue spoke.

But I was past stopping. My finger, frantic inside of me, had the separate persistence of a machine strapped to my body.

"Tell me you're happy. Tell me how happy you are. Tell me you're happy," he crooned over and over again.

"I am I am I am I am I am."

I was afraid the spasms would possess me forever, and when they began to subside and weaken, I shut my eyes and tried for at least one more. After that I couldn't open my eyes. A leaden, an irresistible drowsiness held them closed.

I heard Clarissa ask, "Did you get it on tape?"

"Be quiet, Clarissa."

"Victor should get off behind that. Ahhh," she yawned. "Good night, genius."

I sat up and faced Roger. "You taped it?" I said, hardly able to say or believe my words.

"Oh, Christ, aren't you sleeping?"

"You taped it," I repeated, my eyes swimming with tears. It was as though I'd snapped out of a trance to find myself stark naked, beside a total stranger. My head started to shake. My skin was sticky and cold. I shivered. The chill of the air conditioner penetrated into my bones, and I grabbed for my bundle of clothes. I slipped my T-shirt over my head and frantically forced my clammy legs into my white jeans.

"Easy," Roger said. "Easy, baby. You're wigging. You're undoing all the benefits of untensing your body. Stop beating yourself, Harriet."

"I wish I could beat that tape," I cried, "and forget I ever met you. You drugged me. You planned it all. I know you're all laughing at me, you and your pack of degenerates, so you can drop that act of being so concerned about my tensions." I couldn't look at Roger. All I could think of or see was the seclusion of my solitary cell. I swore to myself that I would never ever again leave it.

Roger grabbed my hand. I knew I was cold, but I didn't realize I was freezing until I felt the warmth of his dry touch. He pulled me down next to him.

"You're like ice. Now, listen to me. I want you to listen to me. You can give me a minute of your time and trust. Be the beautiful, soft, open woman you are. You came like an angel. Smooth and full, you let it all out. I'm proud of you, baby."

"I'm not," I wailed.

"Let me play it back for you, sweetheart. Hear how beautiful you are."

"No," I screamed, covering my ears in self-defense.

"Just listen to it once, for me," he bargained with intensity.

"Never!" I yelled. I could hear Clarissa's nasty chuckle. "How could you," I wailed. "I thought you liked me."

"How could I what?" He stuck to his perplexed act.

"You tricked me," I cried. "It was all arranged. I can't stand it. I've never done anything like that before. You should be locked up. Rapist. Pervert." I wanted to pound my fists against his smooth, hairless chest.

"Stop that racket, Harriet. What is this number you're pulling? You force yourself into my room; you hang in, panting down my neck, snooping around for some action; you have yourself a ball; and then you start screaming bloody murder. What's your game, baby?"

"It wasn't like that," I protested and started to cry.

Shades of Libby fell across my mind. "Oh, God," I heard myself moan.

"Is this how you get your real kicks, with regret, guilt? What the hell is this whole remorse scene about?" Roger demanded. "Let me in on your tragedy."

"You know what you did, you pig."

Roger's voice became softly menacing. "Nobody calls me a pig. Remember that for future reference. And while you're at it, try remembering that nobody forced you into anything. You were raring to go. Is that what the hysteria is about? You think your mama wouldn't approve of her horny little girl? Her baby virgin didn't get permission to jerk off under the covers?"

"Don't say that." I covered my ears again. "I didn't do that. It just happened."

"Got it," Roger snapped back. "That's the scenario. You're alone in your room, minding your own business, and things just happen. You're not even there when they happen. Wow," he said with another shake of his head, "was I taken in by your performance. Congratulations. It's been a long time, many moons, since a chick pulled me into her movie."

"What are you talking about?" I yelled, confusion steaming my brain into a soupy fog. "What does all that garbage have to do with you making a fool of me?" The soup oozed out of my eyes. "Tricking me into making a spectacle of myself to entertain your cronies and some freak called Victor."

"Is this ridiculous fuss about the tape, that erotic

193

masterpiece?" He laughed. "Why, I have tapes and films of Henny Penny climbing the wall that make yours sound like choir practice."

"Henny Penny," I shrieked, "is not my idea of feminine perfection."

"What?" a half-awake voice called out.

"Go back to sleep," Roger told her. "Henny Penny is beautiful," he informed me. "Nothing comes between her and her gratification. You could take a few lessons from her. She's totally in touch with herself, not into some idiotic never-never land where things just happen. She takes charge of what happens, and she takes pleasure, full, uninterrupted pleasure in her scene. That's her trip. She's on an ecstasy trip. It's not for every chick. If you can't make it, Harriet, that's cool. But don't go around asking for it, pretending you're up for it, and then hollering rape. You're not going to make friends that way." He smiled, his teeth a dark band across his pallid face.

He stood up, stretched, and exercised his fingers. He switched off the hanging red bulb. At first I was blind, but then Roger and the room were outlined by a dull gray light coming from the bright, blank television tube. There was also the beginning of daylight, smothered behind the closed drapes. Roger walked to the window and pulled back one of the drapes. A stingy light settled on the chilly, shabby room. I hoped he would turn off the air conditioner, but he didn't.

"We'll have to split soon," Roger mumbled to himself. "It looks like more rain." He came toward me, his white torso glistening, his jeans slipping down his narrow hips. He adjusted them with a pull on his heavy leather belt. He was leaner and taller than my mental picture of him. He sat down in the recliner and lifted the tape machine onto his lap. I watched him, riveted to my place at his feet.

"Here," he said, throwing a spool of brown tape to me. "Catch. A present from me to you. Destroy the evidence and stick to your story that things just happen; or better yet, pretend that nothing happened. Now, take yourself and it out of here."

The tape landed next to me on the worn rug. I couldn't touch it. I couldn't use it. A crazy irrelevancy went through my mind, to wit, that I couldn't play it on a can opener. Claude had a tape recorder. Roger had a tape recorder. Only *I* was lingering in a dead century, with nothing. I thought of the tape recorder I didn't have in the filthy cage across the hall. I strained my mind, trying to recall the significance of the tape. Of course it wasn't the crucial issue. What mattered was the unbearable change in my relationship with Roger. I needed time to explain that to him.

"Fuck off," Roger said, his arms folded sternly in front of him. "What are you waiting for, a military escort?" Instead of time, I was getting an enemy, forcing me out.

I pressed my legs into my body and held on to them as if to protect myself from being knocked over. "Please, Roger, let's talk. I don't want to pretend nothing happened between us. I've had more rapport with you in the past few hours than I've felt in six months, a year, make it five years. Let's discuss it like two adults.

You're not even listening to me." I sobbed. "Please, be fair."

There was a long silence, and a kind of frenzy seized me that Roger wasn't going to grant me an answer. I became almost sick, waiting for an answer.

"Fair," he exploded. "What would be fair in your book, Harriet? If I shot myself? Or would it satisfy you if I took your mindless guilt trip? Suppose I apologize for sitting up all night helping you do your thing and give you my word of honor that nobody will ever hear from my lips that you're a dirty little girl who can't stop whacking off. Will that get me off the hook?"

"Don't," I whispered. "Why are you so angry at me?"

"Why am I angry?" he repeated bitterly. "Should I be a good sport about servicing a cripple, a disaster who barges in here howling for help, and after she's drained my last drop of blood, makes wild accusations about my motives?"

I couldn't defend myself. I felt blindly around my allotted space and located my Marlboros. The crushed pack felt empty, but fortunately it contained two flattened cigarettes. I lit one, and with the first inhale, my heart began to palpitate and some monstrous hand began to shake me.

"Oh, fuck," Roger protested, and I detected an edge of concern in his voice. "I can't believe this chickenshit scene you're laying on me. I can't handle it. Feed me my lines, sweetheart. I don't enjoy hurting you. I know you're not responsible for your insane hang-ups, but I'm only human. I confess, flat out, the workings of your uptight mind are a mystery to me. Tell me what I'm supposed to say and I'll say it. Spell it out for me. Maybe I am being unfair. From where I sit, there are two people arguing. One of them came, the other one didn't, and the one who came is bitching. Do you hate to come?"

"No."

"Look at me when you talk."

"No," I repeated, looking into his face. As the room got lighter, his face got older.

"That's good news. Did my company, my touch, my smell offend you?"

"No," I said promptly, "of course not."

"Well, we're getting somewhere, but don't ask me where," Roger said.

"It's the tape," I said softly, moving cautiously around his explosive temper.

"But I gave you the tape," he said, exasperation resonant in his voice. "Look, there it is next to you, a gift, on the house. Now, can we please adjourn this fucking trial?"

Dawn was becoming daylight. I had a glimmer of what it must feel like to await one's execution.

"Wait," I pleaded. "Stop. It's not the tape. Of course I don't mind about the tape." I couldn't continue. Somewhere near the center of my chest, next to my heart, there was dull, persistent pain that intensified with each breath I took. It was weird, as though a separate, injured creature had taken up residence inside my lungs.

"Hurry it up, Harriet, you have my attention. I wasted an entire evening, but I'm not going to give you the day, too."

"It was the shock." My face hurt from the effort of keeping my head steady.

"What shock?" Roger demanded.

"If you had told me what you were doing while I was trying to . . ." I couldn't complete the thought, much less the statement. Again, the unwelcome tenant squatting in my chest writhed in its independent agony.

"Now, wait a minute, Harriet. You knew what I was doing. You watched me turn the machine on." He leaned forward, his expression tense with controlled rage.

"I didn't," I cried, fighting off a dim memory.

"Baby," he warned me, in a voice hissing with irritation, "I'm trying to get at what's eating you. I believe I'm being extremely patient, but I absolutely draw the line at lying."

"I'm not lying, Roger. I swear, I never lie."

"No, of course not. You don't lie. You just invent. In your fantasy world things either happen or don't happen, depending on which version serves your convenience. I'm nuts, right? That's what you're telling me? It's my imagination. I was dreaming that you watched me turn on the machine."

A shimmering but vivid mirage of Roger bending over the tape recorder flashed between us.

"But that was earlier, for Libby," I said, my remaining shreds of outrage dissolving into frustration and despair.

"And you're claiming that when you took center stage, I turned it off?"

"No, no, no," I protested, "but I forgot."

"Is that why I'm getting the third degree? Because you forgot? Is that the reason for this interrogation? That you have the memory of a three-year-old? Well, answer me, Harriet, or are you running out of paranoid accusations?"

"I can't think when you're so mad at me," I said in a high, thin, unfamiliar voice. "It's just that I thought it was private, between us, and when Clarissa mentioned Victor," I was racing my tears, unable to remember why Clarissa's congratulations had affected me so intensely, "I thought I would die."

"You don't have far to go," Roger said furiously.

I knew then he was never going to forgive me. I had only the vaguest recollection of my crime, but the guilty verdict was clear. Roger sat and watched me. I felt the waves of his contempt crashing into me. I couldn't endure his contempt. I lowered my head to my knees and let the waves engulf me. It was a relief to sink under them. I heard the frantic cries of a drowning person, but I didn't lift my head to look for her. I sank without resistance. Powerful hands reached under my arms and lifted me out of my descent. My rescuer pulled me up onto his lap. I lay against his chest, choking, my lungs bursting. He held my head in the curve of his neck.

"Let it out," he urged me. "Let it go."

Trapped groans filled my throat. I opened my mouth wide to make passage for the bereaved creature inside of me.

"Good, good," Roger's firm voice guided me. "Let the demons out."

My jaw ached. My gaping mouth stretched wider, and an eerie, inhuman sound rushed out of me. It kept coming in an endless stream, as though whatever it was had been coiled tightly around every organ of my body. It pulled itself out of my intestines, crawled through my stomach, slid through my lungs, and it fled, leaving me gasping for air. My head fell loosely against Roger's shoulder, and I became part of the silence in the room. Roger stroked my hair. I breathed in his smell. His skin smelled faintly of ammonia. I felt him tuck my hair carefully behind my ears.

"That was fantastic," he murmured into my ear. "Beautiful, Harriet. I'm proud of you."

I didn't need to speak. I crawled deeper into Roger's lap. His terrible anger was gone. It was like receiving a reprieve after the execution.

"We hardly ever see a breakthrough like that, not behind a thousand milligrams." He rocked me in his arms. "Baby, you let the bad shit out. You're beautiful." He pushed me away from his chest and studied my face. He hugged me. "I see the change in your face. It's fantastic. Do you feel better?"

"Yes," I said, Roger's approval filling me with contentment.

"I'm glad," Roger said. "Baby, I'm sorry you had to

go through so much pain to get there, but you have a lifetime of suffering to get rid of. Your capacity to suffer is proof of your capacity to feel joy. Christ," he said, "what a potential. A few more sessions like this one and you'd soar, like a bird, like a beautiful, radiant, high-flying bird. I knew it," he said, giving vent to his elation, "as soon as you walked into the room. I wasn't asleep. Under all that shame and hostility and lying and aggression is a lovely, vulnerable girl. How will she become whole," he gently shook me, "without a real man to receive her?" He rubbed his knuckles tenderly against my cheek.

"Roger," I said tiredly, "please take me with you." I had no reasons to give him, only a need to be with him. I sat up, balancing myself on the arm of the chair. "I must be with you." I couldn't imagine living outside his arms.

He patted my thigh. "We'll see, Harriet. I'll be back in New York soon, and we'll both think about it."

"No, no, I don't want to think. I'm afraid, I feel in my bones that if we separate, it will be forever. Roger, I must be with you. I can't be alone. What will happen to me?" I clung anxiously to him.

"Don't push, Harriet, I need time to think. I can't impulsively take you to the Institute. Victor wouldn't like that, and he'd be right. The Institute is hard going, expecially for the girls. They are the heart and hands of the Institute. You'd have cooking, farming, cleaning the cabins, and attending with joy to all the needs of the men."

"What else has my life been?" I cried. "Except now

I'd be doing it with a purpose. Roger, please, I need to learn, I want to learn. Take me to the Institute."

"No," he said, "don't question my decisions. I told you, I'll discuss it with Victor. If he agrees, I'll send someone for you. That's why I needed the tape, baby, to convince Victor that you are Institute material. We must be sure you're ready. It's not a hotel you can check in and out of. It's a permanent commitment. No," he said grimly, "I can't risk it."

"Please, Roger, risk it. Take a chance on me. You said I needed a few more sessions. I want to be a bird. I want to fly with you."

"Listen, Harriet, I shouldn't make promises, but I will. I'm grooved by your ability to open up, to rid yourself of poisons. I'll tell that to Victor, which will certainly increase your chances of joining the Institute."

I clasped my hands in front of me. "Oh thank you, Roger."

"Relax." Roger held my clasped hands. "Poor tired baby. You've worked hard tonight. You've earned your rest." He lifted me off his lap and massaged his thighs. "You're a lot of beautiful woman," he said playfully.

I stood mutely in front of him, wondering if I could live through his departure. Roger, with his uncanny sensitivity, understood my problem.

"I made you a promise, Harriet. Trust in me. Your chances are excellent. Now, move. Your blood is going to coagulate. See if you can find my shirt. Henny Penny hung it up somewhere."

It felt as though I had to push the room out of my

way to walk. I found a rough white Mexican shirt hanging on the outside of the closet door.

"Is this it?"

"You're a good girl," he said, pulling it over his head. He shivered. "It's cold in here. Aren't you cold?"

"I think so."

"Well, stop torturing yourself. Turn off the air conditioner."

The air conditioner was an ancient affair, and I examined its mystifying knobs and buttons, uncertainty crawling up my spine. I frantically jerked the plug out of the wall and trotted back to Roger. He had resettled himself in the recliner and was struggling with a pair of suède boots. I sat on my heels and watched him.

"Roger, you do like me, don't you?"

"Baby, I love you." He stamped his foot into the boot.

It was what I expected to hear. "I know," I said softly. Just as I had been battered by the waves of Roger's fury, now I rested in the calm of his love.

He smiled at me, his face haggard over the immaculate white shirt. "Show me what a helpful and obedient girl you can be and wake up Henny Penny, but quietly, don't disturb Clarissa."

I wanted to prolong the intimate moment. I picked up my Marlboros. There was a single squashed but whole cigarette left.

"Don't." Roger took the cigarette from me and tore it into pieces. "Don't smoke." My lips tingled and my fingers twitched. There was nothing left to do but obey him.

Clarissa's negligee and her boy friend's bongo drums lay at the foot of their bed. I moved silently around them. Clarissa slept soundly in her musician's arms, her head cradled on his thin shoulder. I couldn't help but notice what a contented duo they made and thought how sweet it would be if they were buried that way, together, in a shared coffin.

It was no easy matter to make the fine distinction between Henny Penny awake or asleep. Except for the reflexes of her puffy eyelids, her expression remained unchanged. She got up without a murmur, fully attired in her wrinkled Indian mini. She drifted around the room, dopey with sleep.

Roger was busy whispering into the telephone. I caught a few snatches of his conversation. "Heidi loves you, man," and "Sure, I can handle Montreal," and finally, "See you in about five hours."

"Let's get out of here," he said to no one in particular.

"Aren't you too tired for that long drive? Should I make you a cup of coffee?"

"Henny Penny will keep me awake." He gave his faithful dwarf a tight smile. She was occupied with collecting their belongings, meticulously checking out the room. We spotted the tape at the same instant, and I beat her to it.

"Roger," I breathlessly said, holding it out to him, "don't forget the tape."

He refused to receive it. "Give it to Henny Penny."

"She won't lose it or anything?" "I felt a rush of distrust for the inscrutable mule. She was loaded down with a denim jacket and the heavy tape recorder and a canvas bag and a cowboy hat.

"You know," I said timidly, "if I came along with you and waited in the car while you dropped it off for Victor, why we could go on to Montreal together. You wouldn't believe me if I told you how deeply Canada fascinates me."

Roger opened the door. We were all practically tiptoeing in order not to disturb Clarissa. "Don't sweat it, Harriet. I said I'd send for you."

"But when? You know I'll be here only till the twenty-third. Did I mention that? After the twenty-third, I'll be gone, who knows where? Paris? Prague? Rome?"

I was seized with uncertainty, my hysteria mounting to the sound of the elevator creaking slowly up to our floor. Roger kept his finger on the down button, impatiently watching the metal arrow. He spoke without looking at me.

"Don't leave your room except when absolutely necessary. Don't talk to strangers. And don't," he lowered his eyes and glared at me, "don't under any circumstances discuss the Institute with anyone."

It was gratifying to receive orders. My trust in Roger became complete. They stepped into the cubicle, and Roger took the cowboy hat from Henny Penny and put it on his head. His face disappeared under the wide brim.

"I won't tell a soul," I vowed, as the elevator doors slid between us, cutting off our goodbyes.

My cell looked as though an infuriated junkie had torn the place apart, in which case, I could only hope he had an allergy to tuna fish. I lay down on the disheveled cot, numb with fatigue. I opened a fresh pack of Marlboros and stared at the brown and white circles. I had no thoughts, only a dim awareness of myself listening and waiting.

TITLES IN SERIES

For a complete list of titles, visit www.nyrb.com or write to:
Catalog Requests, NYRB, 435 Hudson Street, New York, NY 10014